I0609174

Hugh Stowell Scott

The slave of the lamp

Vol. 1

Hugh Stowell Scott

The slave of the lamp
Vol. 1

ISBN/EAN: 9783744739009

Printed in Europe, USA, Canada, Australia, Japan

Cover: Foto ©Andreas Hilbeck / pixelio.de

More available books at **www.hansebooks.com**

THE SLAVE OF THE LAMP

BY

HENRY SETON MERRIMAN

AUTHOR OF 'YOUNG MISTLEY'

IN TWO VOLUMES

VOL. I.

.

LONDON

SMITH, ELDER, & CO., 15 WATERLOO PLACE

1892

[All rights reserved]

CONTENTS

OF

THE FIRST VOLUME

THE

SLAVE OF THE LAMP

———◆———

CHAPTER I

IN THE RUE ST. GINGOLPHE

IT was, not so many years ago, called the Rue
de l'Empire, but republics are proverbially
sensitive. Once they are established they
become morbidly desirous of obliterating a
past wherein no republic flourished. The
street is therefore dedicated to St. Gingolphe
to-day. To-morrow? Who can tell?

It is presumably safe to take it for granted
that you are located in the neighbourhood of
the Louvre, on the north side of the river

which is so unimportant a factor to Paris.
For all good Englishmen have been, or hope
in the near future to be, located near this spot.
All good Americans, we are told, relegate
the sojourn to a more distant future.

The bridge to cross is that of the Holy
Fathers. So called to-day. Once upon a
time—but no matter. Bridges are peculiarly
liable to change in troubled times. The
Rue St. Gingolphe is situated between the
Boulevard St. Germain and Quai Voltaire.
One hears with equal facility the low-toned
boom of the steamers' whistle upon the river,
and the crack of whips in the boulevard.
Once across the bridge, turn to the right,
and go along the Quay, between the lime-
trees and the bookstalls. You will probably
go slowly because of the bookstalls. No one
worth talking to could help doing so. Then
turn to the left, and after a few paces you

will find upon your right hand the Rue
St. Gingolphe. It is noted in the Directory
'Botot' that this street is one hundred and
forty-five mètres long; and who would care
to contradict 'Botot,' or even to throw the
faintest shadow of a doubt upon his statement? He has probably measured.

If your fair and economical spouse should
think of repairing to the Bon-Marché to
secure some of those wonderful linen pillow-
cases (at one franc forty) with your august
initial embroidered on the centre with a view
of impressing the sleeper's cheek, she will
pass the end of the Rue St. Gingolphe on
her way—provided the cabman be honest.
There! You cannot help finding it now.

The street itself is a typical Parisian
street of one hundred and forty-five mètres.
There is room for a baker's, a café, a boot-
maker's, and a tobacconist who sells very few

stamps. The Parisians do not write many letters. They say they have not time. But the tobacconist makes up for the meanness of his contribution to the inland revenue of one department by a generous aid to the other. He sells a vast number of cigarettes and cigars of the very worst quality. And it is upon the worst quality that the Government makes the largest profit. It is in every sense of the word a weed which grows as lustily as any of its compeers in and around Oran, Algiers, and Bonah.

The Rue St. Gingolphe is within a stone's-throw of the Ecole des Beaux-Arts, and in the very centre of a remarkably cheap and yet respectable quarter. Thus there are many young men occupying apartments in close proximity—and young men do not mind much what they smoke, especially provincial young men living in Paris. They feel it

incumbent upon them to be constantly
smoking something—just to show that they
are Parisians, true sons of the pavement,
knowing how to live. And their brightest
hopes are in all truth realised, because theirs
is certainly a reckless life, flavoured as it is
with 'number one' tobacco, and those 'little
corporal' cigarettes which are enveloped in
the blue paper.

The tobacconist's shop is singularly con-
venient. It has, namely, an entrance at the
back, as well as that giving on to the street
of St. Gingolphe. This entrance is through
a little courtyard, in which is the stable
and coach-house combined, where Madame
Perinère, a lady who paints the magic word
'Modes' beneath her name on the door-post
of number seventeen, keeps the dapper little
cart and pony which carry her bonnets to the
farthest corner of Paris.

The tobacconist is a large man, much given to perspiration. In fact, one may safely make the statement that he perspires annually from the middle of April to the second or even third week in October. In consequence of this habit he wears no collar, and a man without a collar does not start fairly on the social race. It is always best to make inquiries before condemning a man who wears no collar. There is probably a very good reason, as in the case of Mr. Jacquetot, but it is to be feared that few pause to seek it. One need not seek the reason with much assiduity in this instance, because the tobacconist of the Rue St. Gingolphe is always prepared to explain it at length. French people are thus. They talk of things, and take pleasure in so doing, which we, on this side of the Channel, treat with a larger discretion.

Mr. Jacquetot does not even wear a collar

on Sunday, for the simple reason that Sunday
is to him as other days. He attends no place
of worship, because he acknowledges but one
god—the god of most Frenchmen—his inner
man. His pleasures are gastronomical, his
sorrows stomachic. The little shop is open
early and late, Sundays, week-days, and holi-
days. Moreover, the tobacconist—Mr. Jacquetot himself—is always at his post, on the
high chair behind the counter, near the window, where he can see into the street. This
constant attention to business is almost pheno-
menal, because Frenchmen who worship the
god of Mr. Jacquetot love to pay tribute on
fête-days at one of the little restaurants on the
Place at Versailles, at Duval's, or even in the
Palais Royal. Mr. Jacquetot would have loved
nothing better than a pilgrimage to any one of
these shrines, but he was tied to the little
tobacco store. Not by the chains of com-

merce. Oh, no! When rallied by his neighbours for such an unenterprising love of his
own hearth, he merely shrugged his heavy
shoulders.

'What will you?' he would say; 'one has
one's affairs.'

Now the affairs of Mr. Jacquetot were, in
the days with which we have to do, like many
things on this earth, inasmuch as they were
not what they seemed.

It would be inexpedient, for reasons closely
connected with the tobacconist of the Rue St.
Gingolphe, as well as with other gentlemen
still happily with us in the flesh, to be too
exact as to dates. Suffice it, therefore, to say
that it was only a few years ago that Mr.
Jacquetot sat one evening as usual in his little
shop. It happened to be a Tuesday evening,
which is fortunate, because it was on Tues-
days and Saturdays that the little barber from

round the corner called and shaved the vast cheeks of the tobacconist. Mr. Jacquetot was therefore quite presentable—doubly so, indeed, because it was yet March, and he had not yet entered upon his summer season.

The little street was very quiet. There was no through traffic, and folks living in this quarter of Paris usually carry their own parcels. It was thus quite easy to note the approach of any passenger, when such had once turned the corner. Someone was approaching now, and Mr. Jacquetot threw away the stump of a cheap cigar. One would almost have said that he recognised the step at a considerable distance. Young people are in the habit of considering that when one gets old and stout one loses in intelligence; but this is not always the case. One is apt to expect little from a fat man; but that is often a mistake.

Mr. Jacquetot weighed seventeen stone, but he was eminently intelligent. He had recognised the footstep while it was yet seventy mètres away.

In a few moments a gentleman of middle height paused in front of the shop, noted that it was a tobacconist's, and entered, carrying an unstamped letter with some ostentation. It must, by the way, be remembered that in France postage-stamps are to be bought at all tobacconists'.

The new-comer's actions were characterised by a certain carelessness, as if he were going through a formula—perfunctorily—without admitting its necessity.

He nodded to Mr. Jacquetot, and rather a pleasant smile flickered for a moment across his face. He was a singularly well-made man, of medium height, with straight square shoulders and small limbs. He wore spec-

tacles, and as he looked at one straight in the
face there was a singular contraction of the
eyes which hardly amounted to a cast—moreover, it was momentary. It was precisely the
look of a hawk when its hood is suddenly removed in full daylight. This resemblance was
furthered by the fact that the man's profile was
birdlike. He was clean-shaven, and there was
in his sleek head and determined little face
that smooth compact self-complacency which
is to be noted in the head of a hawk.

The face was small, like that of a Greek
bust, but in expression it suggested a yet older
people. There was that mystic depth of expression which comes from ancient Egypt. No
one feature was obtrusive—all were chiselled
with equal delicacy; and yet there was only one
point of real beauty in the entire countenance.
The mouth was perfect. But the man with a
perfect mouth is usually one whom it will be

found expedient to avoid. Without a certain allowance of sensuality no man is genial—without a little weakness there is no kind heart. This Frenchman's mouth was not, however, obtrusively faultless. It was perfect in its design, but, somehow, many people failed to take note of the fact. It is so with the ' many,' one finds. The human world is so blind that at times it would be almost excusable to harbour the suspicion that animals see more. There may be something in that instinct by which dogs, horses, and cats distinguish between friends and foes, detect sympathy, discover antipathy. It is possible that they see things in the human face to which our eyes are blinded—intentionally and mercifully blinded. If some of us were a little more observant, a few of the human combinations which we bring about might perhaps be less egregiously mistaken.

It was probably the form of the lips that
lent pleasantness to the smile with which
Mr. Jacquetot was greeted, rather than the
expression of the velvety eyes, which had in
reality no power of smiling at all.   They were
sad eyes, like those of the women one sees on
the banks of the Upper Nile, which never
alter in expression—eyes that do not seem to
be busy with this life at all, but fully occupied with something else : something beyond
to-morrow or behind yesterday.

'Not yet arrived?' inquired the new-
comer in a voice of some distinction.   It was
a full, rich voice, and the French it spoke was
not the French of Mr. Jacquetot, nor, indeed,
of the Rue St. Gingolphe.   It was the language one sometimes hears in an old *château*
lost in the depths of the country—the vast
unexplored rural districts of France—where
the bearers of dangerously historical names

live out their lives with a singular suppression and patience. They are either biding their time or else they are content with the past and the part played by their ancestors therein. For there is an old French and a new. In Paris the new is spoken—the very newest. Were it anything but French it would be intolerably vulgar; as it is, it is merely neat and intensely expressive.

'Not yet arrived, sir,' said the tobacconist, and then he seemed to recollect himself, for he repeated :

'Not yet arrived,' without the respectful addition which had slipped out by accident.

The new arrival took out his watch—a small one of beautiful workmanship, the watch of a lady—and consulted it. His movements were compact and rapid. He would have made a splendid light-weight boxer.

'That,' he said shortly, 'is the way they fail. They do not understand the necessity of exactitude. The people—see you, Mr. Jacquetot, they fail because they have no exactitude.'

'But I am of the people,' moving ponderously on his chair.

'Essentially so. I know it, my friend. But I have taught you something.'

The tobacconist laughed.

'I suppose so. But is it safe to stand there in the full day? Will you not pass in? The room is ready; the lamp is lighted. There is an agent of the police always at the end of the street now.'

'Ah, bah!' and he shrugged his shoulders contemptuously. 'I am not afraid of them. There is only one thing to be feared, Citizen Jacquetot—the press. The press and the people, *bien entendu*.'

'If you despise the people why do you use them?' asked Jacquetot abruptly.

'In default of better, my friend. If one has not steam one uses the river to turn the mill-wheel. The river is slow; sometimes it is too weak, sometimes too strong. One never has full control over it, but it turns the wheel —it turns the wheel, brother Jacquetot.'

'And eventually sweeps away the miller,' suggested the tobacconist lightly. It must be remembered that though stout he was intelligent. Had he not been so it is probable that this conversation would never have taken place. The dark-eyed man did not look like one who would have the patience to deal with stupid people.

Again the pleasant smile flickered like the light of a fire in a dark place.

'That,' was the reply, 'is the affair of the miller.'

'But,' conceded Jacquetot, meditatively selecting a new cigar from a box which he had reached without moving from his chair, 'but the people—they are fools, hein!'

'Ah!' with a protesting shrug, as if deprecating the enunciation of such a platitude.

Then he passed through into a little room behind the shop—a little room where no daylight penetrated, because there was no window to it. It depended for daylight upon the shop, with which it communicated by a door of which the upper half was glass. But this glass was thickly curtained with the material called Turkey-red, threefold.

And the tobacconist was left alone in his shop, smoking gravely. There are some people like oysters, inasmuch as they leave an after-taste behind them. The man who had just gone into the little room at the rear of the tobacconist's shop of the Rue St. Gingolphe in Paris was one of these. And the taste he left behind him was rather disquieting. One was apt to feel that there was a mistake somewhere in the ordering of human affairs, and that this man was one of its victims.

In a few minutes two men passed hastily through the shop into the little room, with scarcely so much as a nod for Mr. Jacquetot.

CHAPTER II

TOOLS

THE first man to enter the room was clad in a blouse of coarse grey cloth which reached down to his knees. On his head he wore a black silk cap, very much pressed down and exceedingly greasy on the right side. This was to be accounted for by the fact that he used his right shoulder more than the left in that state of life in which he had been placed. It was not what we, who do not kill, would consider a pleasant state. He was, in fact, a slayer of beasts—a foreman at the slaughter-house.

It is, perhaps, fortunate that Antoine

Lerac is of no great prominence in this record, and of none in his official capacity at the slaughter-house. But the man is worthy of some small attention, because he was so essentially of the nineteenth century—so distinctly a product of the latter end of what is, for us at least, the most important cycle of years the world has passed through. He was a man wearing the blouse with ostentation, and glorying in the greasy cap : professing his unwillingness to exchange the one for an ermine robe or the other for a crown. As a matter of fact, he invariably purchased the largest and roughest blouse to be found, and his cap was unnecessarily soaked with suet. He was a knight of industry of the very worst description—a braggart, a talker, a windbag. He preached, or rather he shrieked, the doctrine of equality, but the equality he sought was that which would place him on a par with his superiors, while in no way benefiting those beneath him.

At one time, when he had first come into contact with the dark-eyed man who now sat at the table watching him curiously, there had been a struggle for mastery.

'I am,' he had said with considerable heat, 'as good as you. That is all I wish to demonstrate.'

'No,' replied the other with that calm and assured air of superiority which the people once tried in vain to stamp out with the guillotine. 'No, it is not. You want to demonstrate that you are superior, and you cannot do it. You say that you have as much right to walk on the pavement as I. I admit it. In your heart you want to prove that you have *more*, and you cannot do it. I could wear your blouse with comfort, but you could not put on my hat or my gloves

without making yourself ridiculous. But—
that is not the question. Let us get to
business.'

And in time the butcher succumbed, as
he was bound to do, to the man whom he
shrewdly suspected of being an aristocrat.

He who entered the room immediately
afterwards was of a very different type. His
mode of entry was of another description.
Whereas the man of blood swaggered in with
an air of nervous truculence, as if he were
afraid that someone was desirous of disputing
his equality, the next comer crept in softly,
and closed the door with accuracy. He was
the incarnation of benevolence—in the best
sense of the word, a sweet old man—looking
out upon the world through large tinted
spectacles with a beam which could not be
otherwise than blind to all motes. In earlier
years his face might, perhaps, have been a

trifle hard in its contour ; but Time, the lubricator, had eased some of the corners, and it was now the seat of kindness and love. He bowed ceremoniously to the first comer, and his manner seemed rather to breathe of fraternity than equality. As he bowed he mentioned the gentleman's name in such loving tones that no greeting could have been heartier.

'Citizen Morot,' he said.

The butcher, with more haste than dignity, assumed the chair which stood at the opposite end of the table to that occupied by the Citizen Morot. He had evidently hurried in first in order to secure that seat. From his pocket he produced a somewhat soiled paper, which he threw with exaggerated carelessness across the table. His manner was not entirely free from a suggestion of patronage.

'What have we here?' inquired the first comer, who had not hitherto opened his lips, with a deep interest which might possibly have been ironical. He was just the sort of man to indulge in irony for his own satisfaction. He unfolded the paper, raised his eyebrows, and read.

'Ah!' he said, 'a receipt for five hundred rifles with bayonets and shoulder-straps complete. "Received of the Citizen Morot five hundred rifles with bayonets and shoulder-straps complete.—Antoine Lerac."'

He folded the paper again and carefully tore it into very small pieces.

'Thank you,' he said gravely.

Then he turned in his chair and threw the papers into the ash-tray of the little iron stove behind him.

'I judged it best to be strictly business-like,' said the butcher, with moderately well-simulated carelessness.

' But yes, Monsieur Lerac,' with a shrug. ' We of the Republic distrust each other so completely.'

The old gentleman looked from one to the other with a soothing smile.

' The brave Lerac,' he said, ' is a man of business.'

Citizen Morot ignored this observation.

' And,' he said, turning to Lerac, ' you have them stored in a safe place ? There is absolutely no doubt of that ? '

' Absolutely none.'

' Good.'

' They are under my own eye.'

' Very good. It is not for a short time only, but for some months. One cannot hurry the people. Besides, we are not ready.

The rifles we bought, the ammunition we must steal.'

'They are good rifles—they are English,' said the butcher.

'Yes; the English Government is full of chivalry. They are always ready to place it within the power of their enemies to be as well armed as themselves.'

The old gentleman laughed—a pleasant, cooing laugh. He invariably encouraged humour, this genial philanthropist.

'At last Friday's meeting,' Lerac said shortly, 'we enrolled forty new members. We now number four hundred and two in our *arrondissement* alone.'

'Good,' muttered the Citizen Morot, without enthusiasm.

'And four hundred hardy companions they are.'

'So I should imagine' (very gravely).

'Four hundred strong men,' broke in the old gentleman, rather hastily. 'Ah, but that is already a power.'

'It is,' opined Lerac sententiously, 'the strong man who is the power. Riches are nothing; birth is nothing. This is the day of force. Force is everything.'

'Everything,' acquiesced Morot, fervently. He was consulting a small note-book, wherein he jotted down some figures.

'Four hundred and two,' he muttered as he wrote, 'up to Friday night, in the *arrondissement* of the citizen—the good citizen —Antoine Lerac.'

The butcher looked up with a doubtful expression upon his coarse face. His great brutal lips twitched, and he was on the point of speaking when the Citizen Morot's velvety eyes met his gaze with a quiet smile in which arrogance and innocence were mingled.

'And now,' said the last-mentioned, turning affably to the old gentleman, 'let us have the report of the reverend Father.'

'Ah,' laughed Lerac, without attempting to conceal the contempt that was in his soul, ' the Church.'

The old gentleman spread out his hands in mild deprecation.

'Yes,' he admitted, 'we are under a shadow. I do not even dare to wear my cassock.'

'You are in a valley of shadow, my reverend friend,' said the butcher, with visible exultation, 'to which the sun will never penetrate now.'

The Citizen Morot laughed at this pleasantry, while the old man against whom it was directed bowed his head patiently.

'And yet,' said the laugher, with a certain air of patronage, 'the Church is of some use still. She paid for those rifles, and she will pay for the ammunition—is it not so, my father?'

'Without doubt—without doubt.'

'Not to mention,' continued the other, ' many contributions towards our general fund. The force that is supplied by the strong right arm of the people is, one finds, a force constantly in need of substantial replenishment.'

' But,' exclaimed the butcher, emphatically banging his fist down upon the table, ' why does she do it? That is what I want to know ! '

The old priest glanced furtively towards Morot, and then his face assumed an air of childish bewilderment.

' Ah ! ' he said guilelessly, ' who can tell ? '

' Who, indeed ! ' chimed in Morot.

The butcher was pleased with himself.

He sat upright, and, banging the table a second time, he looked round defiantly.

'But,' said Morot, in an indifferent way which was frequently characteristic, 'I do not see that it matters much. The money is good. It buys rifles, and it places them in the hands of the Citizen Lerac and his hardy companions. And when all is said and done, when the cartridges are burnt and a New Commune is raised, what does it matter whose money bought the rifles, and with what object the money was supplied?'

The old gentleman looked relieved. He was evidently of a timid and conciliatory nature, and would, with slight encouragement, have turned upon that Church of which he was the humble representative, merely for the sake of peace.

The butcher cleared his throat after the

manner of the streets—causing Morot to wince visibly—and acquiesced.

'But,' he added cunningly, 'the Church, see you—Ach! it is deep—it is treacherous. Never trust the Church!'

The Citizen Morot, to whom these remarks were addressed, smiled in a singular way and made no reply. Then he turned gravely to the old man and said,

'Have you nothing to report to us—my father?'

'Nothing of great importance,' replied he, humbly. 'All is going on well. We are in treaty for two hundred rifles with the Montenegrin Government, and shall no doubt carry the contract through. I go to England next week in order to carry out the—the—what shall I say?—the loan of the ammunition.'

'Ha, ha!' laughed the butcher.

Morot smiled also, as he made an entry in the little note-book.

'Next week?' he said, interrogatively.

'Yes—on Tuesday.'

'Thank you.'

The butcher here rose and ostentatiously dragged out a watch from the depths of his blouse.

'I must go,' he said. 'I have committee at seven o'clock.   And I shall dine first.'

'Yes,' said Morot, gravely. 'Dine first. Take good care of yourself, citizen.'

'Trust me.'

'I do,' was the reply, delivered with a little nod in answer to Lerac's curt farewell bow.

The butcher walked noisily through the shop—heavy with responsibility—weighted with the sense of his own importance to the world in general and to France in particular.

Had he walked less noisily he might have overheard the soft laugh of the old priest.

Citizen Morot did not laugh. He was not a laughing man. But a fine, disdainful smile passed over his face, scarce lighting it up at all.

'What an utter fool the man is!' he said impatiently.

'Yes—sir,' replied the old man, 'but if he were less so it would be difficult to manage him.'

'I am not sure. I always prefer to deal with knaves than with fools.'

'That is because your Highness knows how to outwit them.'

'No titles—my father,' said the Citizen Morot, quietly. 'No titles here, if you please. Tell me, are you quite sure of this scum— this Lerac?'

'As sure as one can be of anything

that comes from the streets. He is an ex-
citable, bumptious, quarrelsome man; but he
has a certain influence with those beneath
him, although it seems hard to realise that
there are such.'

'Ha! you are right! But a republic is a
social manure-heap—that which is on the top
is not pleasant, and the stuff below—ugh!'

The manner of the two men had quite
changed. He who was called Morot leant
back in his seat and stretched his arms out
wearily. There is no disguise like animation;
when that is laid aside we see the real man or
the real woman. In repose this Frenchman
was not cheerful to look upon. He was not
sanguine, and a French pessimist is the worst
thing of the kind that is to be found.

When the door had closed behind the
departing Lerac, the old priest seemed to
throw off suddenly quite a number of years.

His voice, when next he spoke, was less senile, his movements were brisker. He was, in a word, less harmless.

Mr. Jacquetot had finished his dinner, brought in from a neighbouring restaurant all hot, and was slumberously enjoying a very strong-smelling cigar, when the door of the little room opened at length, and the two men went out together into the dimly-lighted street.

CHAPTER III

WITHOUT REST

HALFWAY down Fleet Street, on the left-hand side, stands the church of St. Dunstan-in-the West. Around its grimy foundations there seethes a struggling, toiling race of men— not only from morning till night, but throughout the twenty-four hours. Within sound of this church bell a hundred printing-presses throb out their odorous broadsheets to be despatched to every part of the world. Day and night, week in week out, the human writing-machines, and those other machines which are almost human (and better than human in some points) hurry through their allotted tasks, and ignore the saintly shadow cast upon them by the spire of St. Dunstan. This is indeed the centre of the world : the hub from whence spring the spokes of the vast wheel of life. For to this point all things over the world converge by a vast web of wire, railroad, coach road, and steamer track. Upon wings that boast of greater speed than the wind can compass come to this point the voices of our kin in farthest lands. News—news—news. News from the East of events occurring in the afternoon—scan it over and flash it westward, where it will be read on the morning of the same day! News in every tongue to be translated and brought into shape—while the solemn church clock tells his tale in deep voice, audible above the din and scurry.

From hurried scribbler to pale compositor, and behold, the news is bawled all over London! Such work as this goes on for ever around the church of St. Dunstan. Scribblers come and scribblers go ; compositors come to their work young and hopeful, they leave it bent and poisoned, yet the work goes on. Each day the pace grows quicker, each day some new means of rapid propagation is discovered, and each day life becomes harder to live. One morning, perhaps, a scribbler is absent from his post—'Brain-fever, complete rest ; a wreck.' For years his writings have been read by thousands daily. A new man takes the vacant chair—he has been waiting more or less impatiently for this— and the thousands are none the wiser. One night the head compositor presses his black hand to his sunken chest, and staggers home. 'And time too—he's had his turn,' mutters the second compositor as he thinks of the extra five shillings a week. No doubt he is right. Every dog his day.

Nearly opposite to the church stands a tall narrow house of dirty red brick, and it is with this house that we have to do.

At seven o'clock, one evening some years ago—when heads now grey were brown, when eyes now dim were bright—the Strand was in its usual state of turmoil. Carriage followed carriage. Seedy clerks hustled past portly merchants—not their own masters, *bien entendu*, but those of other seedy clerks. Carriages and foot-passengers were alike going westward. All were leaving behind them the day and the busy city—some after a few hours devoted to the perusal of 'Times' and 'Gazette'; others fagged and weary from a long day of dusty books.

Ah! those were prosperous days in the City. Days when men of but a few years'

standing rolled out to Clapham or Highgate
behind a pair of horses. Days when books
were often represented by a bank-book and a
roughly-kept day-book. What need to keep
mighty ledgers when profits are great and
returns quick in their returning?

As the pedestrians made their way along
the narrow pavement, some of them glanced
at the door of the tall red-brick house and
read the inscription on a brass-plate screwed
thereon. This consisted of two mystic words:
'The Beacon.' There was, however, in
reality, no mystery about it. The 'Beacon'
was a newspaper, published weekly, and the
clock of St. Dunstan's striking seven told the
end of another week. The publishing day
was past; another week with its work and
pleasure was to be faced.

From early morning until six o'clock in
the evening this narrow doorway and passage

had been crowded by a heaving, swearing, laughing mass of more or less dilapidated humanity interested in the retail sale of newspapers. At six o'clock Ephraim Bander, a retired constable, now on the staff of the 'Beacon,' had taken his station at the door, in order to greet would-be purchasers with the laconic and discouraging words: 'Sold hout!'

During the last two years ex-constable Bander had announced the selling 'hout' of the 'Beacon' every Tuesday evening.

At seven o'clock Mrs. Bander emerged from her den on the fourth floor, like a portly good-natured spider, and with a broom proceeded to attack the dust shaken from the boots of the journalistic fraternity, with noisy energy. After that she polished the doorplate; and peace reigned within the narrow house.

On the second floor there was a small room with windows looking out into a narrow lane behind the house. It was a singularly quiet room ; the door opened and shut without sound or vibration ; double windows ensured immunity from the harrowing cries of such enterprising merchants as exercised their lungs and callings in the narrow lane beneath. À certain sense of ease and comfort imperceptibly crept over the senses of persons entering this tiny apartment. It must have been in the atmosphere ; for some rooms more luxuriously furnished are without it. It certainly does not lie in the furniture— this imperceptible sense of companionship ; it does not lurk in the curtains. Some mansions know it, and many cottages. It is even to be met with in the tiny cabin of a coasting vessel.

This diminutive room, despite its lack of

sunlight, was such as one might wish to sit in. A broad low table stood in the middle of the floor, and on it lay the mellow light of a shaded lamp. At this table two men were seated opposite to each other. One was writing, slowly and easily, the other was idling with the calm restfulness of a man who has never worked very hard. He was rolling his pencil up to the top of his blotting-pad, and allowing it to come down again in accordance with the rules of gravity.

This was Mr. Bodery's habit when thoughtful; and after all, there was no great harm in it. Mr. Bodery was editor and proprietor of the 'Beacon.' The amusing and somewhat satirical article which appeared weekly under the heading of 'Light' was penned by the chubby hand at that moment engaged with the pencil.

Mr. Morgan, sub-editor, was even stouter

than his chief. Laughter was his most prominent characteristic. He laughed over ' Light ' when in its embryo state, he laughed when the ' Beacon ' sold out at six o'clock on Tuesday evenings. He laughed when the printing-machine went wrong on Monday afternoon, and—most wonderful of all—he laughed at his own jokes, in which exercise he was usually alone. His jokes were not of the first force. Mr. Morgan was the author of the slightly laboured and weighty Parliamentary articles on the first page. He never joked on paper, which is a gift apart.

These two gentlemen were in no way of brilliant intellect. They had their share of sound, practical common-sense, which is in itself a splendid substitute. Fortune had come to them (as it comes to most men when it comes at all) without any apparent reason. Mr. Bodery had supplied the capital, and

Mr. Morgan's share of the undertaking was added in the form of a bustling, hollow energy. The 'Beacon' was lighted, so to speak. It burnt in a dull and somewhat flickering manner for some years; then a new hand fed the flame, and its light spread afar.

It was from pure good nature that Mr. Bodery held out a helping hand to the son of his old friend, Walter Vellacott, when that youth appeared one day at the office of the 'Beacon,' and in an off-hand manner announced that he was seeking employment. Like many actions performed from a similar motive, Mr. Bodery's kindness of heart met with its reward. Young Christian Vellacott developed a remarkable talent for journalistic literature—in fact, he was fortunate enough to have found, at the age of twenty-two, his avocation in life.

Gradually, as the years wore on, the influence of the young fellow's superior intellect made itself felt. From the position of a mere supernumerary, he worked his way upwards, taking on to his shoulders one duty after another—bearing the weight, quietly and confidently, of one responsibility after another. This exactly suited Mr. Bodery and his subeditor. There was very little of the slave in the composition of either. They delighted in an easy, luxurious life, with just enough work to impart a pleasant feeling of self-satisfaction. It suited Christian Vellacott also. In a few weeks he found his level—in a few months he began rising to higher levels.

He was an only son; the only child of a brilliant father whose name was known in every court in Europe as that of a harum-scarum diplomatist, who could have done great things in his short life if he had wished to. It is from only sons that fortune selects her favourites. Men who have no brothers to share their amusements turn to serious matters early in life. Christian Vellacott soon discovered that a head was required at the office of the ' Beacon ' to develop the elements of success undoubtedly lying within the journal, and that the owner of such a head could in time dictate his own terms to the easy-going proprietor.

Unsparingly he devoted the whole of his exceptional energies to the work before him. He lived in and for it. Each night he went home fagged and weary ; but each morning saw him return to it with undaunted spirit.

Human nature, however, is exhaustible. The influence of a strong mind over a strong body is great, but it is nevertheless limited. The ' Beacon ' had reached a large circulation, but its slave was worn out. Two years without a holiday—two years of hurried hard brain-work had left their mark. It is often so when a man finds his avocation too early. He is too hurried, works too hard, and collapses; or he becomes self-satisfied, over-confident, and unbearable. Fortunately for Christian Vellacott he was devoid of conceit, which is like the scaffolding round a church-spire, reaching higher and falling first.

There was also a 'home' influence at work. When Christian passed out of the narrow door-way, and turned his face westward, his day's work was by no means over, as will be shown hereafter.

As Mr. Bodery rolled his pencil up and down his blotting pad, he was slowly realising the fact that something must be done. Presently he looked up, and his pleasant eyes rested on the bent head of his sub-editor.

'Morgan,' he said, 'I have been thinking—— Seems to me Vellacott wants a
rest! He's played out!'

Mr. Morgan wiped his pen vigorously upon
his coat, just beneath the shoulder, and sat
back in his chair.

'Yes,' he replied; 'he has not been up to
the mark for some time. But you will find
difficulty in making him take a holiday. He
is a devil for working—ha, ha!'

This 'ha, ha!' did not mean very much.
There was no mirth in it. It was a species of
punctuation, and implied that Mr. Morgan had
finished his remark.

'I will ring for him now and see what he
ays about it.'

Mr. Bodery extended his chubby white
hand and touched a small gong. Almost in-
stantaneously the silent door opened and a
voice from without said, 'Yess'r.' A small

boy with a mobile wicked mouth stood at attention in the doorway.

'Has Mr. Vellacott gone?'

'No—sir!' In a tone which seemed to ask: 'Now *is* it likely?'

'Where is he?'

'In the shop, sir.'

'Ask him to come here, please.'

'Yess'r.'

The small boy closed the door. Once outside he placed his hand upon his heart and made a low bow to the handle, retreating backwards to the head of the stairs. Then he proceeded to slide down the banister, to the trifling detriment of his waistcoat. As he reached the end of his perilous journey a door opened at the foot of the stairs, and a man's form became discernible in the dim light

'Is that the way you generally come down-stairs, Wilson?' asked a voice.

'It is the quickest way, sir!'

'Not quite; there is one quicker, which you will discover some day if you overbalance at the top!'

'Mr. Bodery wishes to see you, please sir!' The small boy's manner was very different from what it had been outside the door up-stairs.

'All right,' replied Vellacott, putting on the coat he had been carrying over his arm. A peculiar smooth rapidity characterised all his movements. At school he had been con-sidered a very 'clean' fielder. The cleanness was there still.

The preternaturally sharp boy—sharp as only London boys are—watched the lithe form vanish up the stairs; then he wagged his head very wisely and said to himself in a patronising way :

'He's the right sort, he is—no chalk there !'

Subsequently he balanced his diminutive person full length upon the balustrade, and proceeded to haul himself laboriously, hand over hand, to the top.

In the meantime Christian Vellacott had passed into the editor's room. The light of the lamp was driven downwards upon the table, but the reflection of it rose and illuminated his face. It was a fairly handsome face, with eyes just large enough to be keen and quick without being dreamy. The slight fair moustache was not enough to hide the mouth, which was refined, and singularly immobile. He glanced at Mr. Bodery, as he entered, quickly and comprehensively, and then turned his eyes towards Mr. Morgan.

His face was very still and unemotional, but it was pale, and his eyes were deeply sunken. A keen observer would have noticed, in comparing the three men, that there was something about the youngest which was lacking in his elders. It lay in the direct gaze of his eyes, in the carriage of his head, in the small, motionless mouth. It was what is vaguely called 'power.'

'Sit down, Vellacott,' said Mr. Bodery. 'We want to have a consultation.' After a short pause he continued: 'You know, of course, that it is a dull season just now. People do not seem to read the papers in August. Now, we want you to take a holiday. Morgan has been away; I shall go when you come back. Say three weeks or a month. You've been overworking yourself a bit—burning the candle at both ends, eh?'

'Hardly at both ends,' corrected Vellacott, with a ready smile which entirely transformed his face. 'Hardly at both ends—at one end in a draught, perhaps.'

'Ha, ha! Very good,' chimed in Mr. Morgan the irrepressible. 'At one end in a draught—that is like me, only the draught has got inside my cheeks and blown them out instead of in like yours, eh? Ha, ha!' And he patted his cheeks affectionately.

'I don't think I care for a holiday just now, thanks,' he said slowly, without remembering to call up a smile for Mr. Morgan's benefit. Unconsciously he put his hand to his forehead, which was damp with the heat of the printing-office which he had just left.

'My dear fellow,' said Mr. Bodery gravely, emphasising his remarks with the pencil, 'you have one thing in life to learn yet—no doubt you have many, but this one in particular you must learn. Work is not the only thing we are created for—not the only thing worth living for. It is a necessary evil, that is all. When you have reached my age you will come to look upon it as such. A little enjoyment is good for everyone. There are many things to form a brighter side to life. Nature —travelling—riding—rowing——'

' And love,' suggested the sub-editor, placing his hand dramatically on the right side of his broad waistcoat instead of the left. He could afford to joke on the subject now that the grass grew high in the little country churchyard where he had laid his young wife fifteen years before. In those days he was a grave, self-contained man, but that sorrow had entirely changed his nature. The true William Morgan only came out on paper now.

Mr. Bodery was right. Christian had yet

to learn a great lesson, and unconsciously he was even now beginning to grasp its meaning. His whole mind was full of his work, and out of those earnest grey eyes his soul was looking at the man who was perhaps saving his life.

'We can easily manage it,' said the editor, continuing his advantage. 'I will take over the foreign policy article. The reviewing you can do yourself, as we can always send you the books, and there is no pressing hurry about them. The general work we will manage somehow—won't we, Morgan?'

'Of course we will; as well as and perhaps better than he could do it himself, eh? Ha, ha!'

'But seriously, Vellacott,' continued Mr. Bodery, 'things will go on just as well for a time. When I was young I used to make that mistake too. I thought that no one could manage things like myself, but in time I realised (as you will do some day) that things went on as smoothly when I was away. Depend upon it, my boy, when a man is put on the shelf, worn out and useless, another soon fills his place. You are too young to go on the shelf yet. To please me, Vellacott, go away for three weeks.'

'You are very kind, sir——' began the young fellow, but Mr. Bodery interrupted him.

'Well, then, that is settled. Shall we say this day week? That will give you time to make your plans.'

With a few words of thanks Christian left the room. Vaguely and mechanically he wandered upstairs to his own particular den. It was a disappointing little chamber. The chaos one expects to find on the desk of a literary man was lacking here. No papers lay on the table in artistic disorder. The presiding genius of the room was method— clear-headed, practical method. The walls were hidden by shelves of books, from the last half-hysterical production of some vain woman to the single-volume work of a man's lifetime. Many of the former were uncut, the latter bore signs of having been read and studied. The companionship of these silent friends brought peace and contentment to the young man's spirit. He sat wearily down, and, leaning his chin upon his folded arms, he thought. Gradually there came into his mind pictures of the fair open country, of rolling hills and quiet valleys, of quiet lanes and running waters. A sudden yearning to breathe God's pure air took possession of his faculties. Mr. Bodery had gained the day. In the room below Mr. Morgan wrote on in his easy, comfortable manner. The editor was still thoughtfully playing with his pencil. The sharp little boy was standing on his head in the passage. At last Mr. Bodery rose from his chair and began his preparations for leaving. As he brushed his hat he looked towards his companion and said :

'That young fellow is worth you and me rolled into one.'

'I recognised that fact some years ago, replied the sub-editor, wiping his pen on his coat. 'It is humiliating, but true. Ha, ha!'

CHAPTER IV

BURDENED

CHRISTIAN VELLACOTT soon descended the
dingy stairs and joined the westward-wending
throng in the Strand. In the midst of the
crowd he was alone, as townsmen soon learn
to be. The passing faces, the roar of traffic,
and the thousand human possibilities of interest around him in no way disturbed his
thoughts. In his busy brain the traffic of
thought, passing and repassing, crossing and
recrossing, went on unaffected by outward
things. A modern poet has confessed that
his muse loves the pavement—a bold confession, but most certainly true. Why does

talent gravitate to cities? Because there it works its best—because friction necessarily produces brilliancy. Nature is a great deceiver; she draws us on to admire her insinuating charms, and in the contemplation of them we lose our energy.

Christian had been born and bred in cities. The din and roar of life was to him what the voice of the sea is to the sailor. In the midst of crowded humanity he was in his element, and as he walked rapidly along he made his way dexterously through the narrow places without thinking of it. While meditating deeply he was by no means absorbed. In his active life there had been no time for thoughts beyond the present, no leisure for dreaming. He could not afford to be absent-minded. Numbers of men are so situated. Their minds are required at all moments, in full working order, clear and rapid—ready, shoes on feet and staff in hand, to go whithersoever they may be called.

Although he was going to the saddest home that ever hung like a mill-stone round a young neck, Christian wasted no time. The glory of the western sky lay ruddily over the river as he emerged from the small streets behind Chelsea and faced the broad placid stream. Presently he stopped opposite the door of a small red-brick house, which formed the corner of a little terrace facing the river and a quiet street running inland from it.

With a latch-key he admitted himself noiselessly—almost surreptitiously. Once inside, he closed the door without unnecessary sound and stood for some moments in the dark little entrance-hall, apparently listening.

Presently a voice broke the silence of

the house. A querulous high-pitched voice,
quavering with the palsy of extreme age.
The sound of it was no new thing for
Christian Vellacott. To-night his lips gave a
little twist of pain as he heard it. The door
of the room on the ground floor was open,
and he could hear the words distinctly
enough.

'You know, Mrs. Strawd, we have a
nephew, but he is always gadding about, I am
sure; he has been a terrible affliction to us.
A frothy, good-for-nothing boy—that is what
he is. We have not set eyes on him for a
month and more. Why, I almost forget his
name!'

'Christian, that is his name—a most
inappropriate one, I am sure,' chimed in
another voice, almost identical in tone.
'Why Walter should have given him such a
name I cannot tell. Ah! sister Judith, things

are different from what they used to be when we were younger!'

The frothy one outside the door seemed in no great degree impressed by these impartial views upon himself, though the pained look was still upon his lips as he turned to hang up his hat.

'He's coming home to night, though, Miss Judith,' said another voice, in a coaxing, wheedling tone, such as one uses towards petulant children. 'He's coming home to-night, sure enough!' It was a pleasant voice, with a strong, capable ring about it. One instinctively felt that the possessor of it was a woman to be relied upon at a crisis.

'Is he now—is he now?' said the first speaker reflectively. 'Well, I am sure it is time he did. We will just give him a lesson, eh, sister Hester?—we will give him a lesson, shall we not?'

At this moment the door opened, and a little woman, quiet though somewhat anxious looking, came out. She evinced no surprise at the sight of the good-for-nothing nephew in the dimly-lighted passage, greeting him in a low voice.

'How have they been to-day, nurse?' he asked.

'Oh, they have been well enough, Master Christian,' was the reply, in a cheerful under-tone. 'Aunt Judith has most got rid of her cold. But they've been very trying, sir—just like children, as wilful as could be—the same question over and over again till I was fit to cry. They are quieter now, but—but it's you they're abusing now, Master Chris!'

The young fellow looked down into the little woman's face. His eyes were sympathetic enough, but he said nothing. With a little nod and a suppressed sigh he turned away from her. He laid his hand upon the door and then stopped.

'As soon as you have brought up tea,' he said, looking back, 'I will take them for the evening, and you can have your rest as usual.'

From the room came, at intervals, the ring of silver, as if someone were moving the spoons and forks from the table. Christian waited until these sounds had ceased before he entered.

'Good evening, Aunt Judith. Good evening, Aunt Hester,' he said cheerily.

They were exactly alike, these two old ladies; the same marvellously wrinkled features and silver hair; voluminous caps and white woollen shawls identical. With exaggerated marks of respect he kissed each by turn on her withered cheek.

'May I sit down, Aunt Judith?' he asked,

and without waiting for an answer drew a chair towards the fireplace, where a small fire burnt though it was the month of August.

'Yes, Nephew Vellacott, you may take a seat,' replied Aunt Judith with chill severity, 'and you may also tell us where you have been during the last four weeks.'

Poor old human wreck! Only ten hours earlier her nephew had bid her farewell for the day. Christian began an explanation in a weary, mechanical way, like an actor tired of the part assigned to him, but the old ladies would not listen. Aunt Hester interrupted him promptly.

'Your shallow excuses are wasted on us, Nephew Vellacott. You have doubtless been away, enjoying yourself and leaving us—us who support you and deprive ourselves in order to keep a decent coat upon your back

—leaving us to the mercy of all the thieves in London. And tell us, pray—what are we to do for spoons and forks to-night?'

'What?' exclaimed Christian with perfunctory interest, 'have the spoons gone——?' he almost said 'again,' but checked himself in time. He turned to look at the table, which had been carefully denuded of every piece of silver.

'There, you see!' quavered Aunt Judith triumphantly; and the two old ladies rubbed their hands, nodded their palsied old heads at each other, and chuckled in utter delight at their nephew's discomfiture, until Aunt Judith was attacked by a violent fit of coughing, which seemed to be tearing her to pieces. Christian watched her with the ready keenness of a sick-nurse.

'How did it occur?' he asked, when the old lady had recovered.

'There, you see,' remarked Aunt Hester, with the precise intonation of her accomplice.

'I *am* sure!' panted Aunt Judith triumphantly.

'I *am* sure!' echoed Aunt Hester.

They allowed their nephew's remorse full scope, and then proceeded laboriously to extract the missing articles from the side of Aunt Judith's arm-chair. This farce was rehearsed every night, nearly word for word. A pleasant recreation for an intellectual man, assuredly. The only relief to the monotony was the occasional loss of a spoon in the crevice between the arm and the seat of Aunt Judith's chair. Then followed such a fumbling and a 'dear me-ing' until the worthless nephew was perforce called to the rescue, to fish and probe with a paper-knife till the lost treasure was recovered.

'We only wished, Nephew Vellacott, to

show you what might have happened during your unconscionable absence. Servants are only too ready to talk to the first comer of their mistresses' wealth and position. They have no discrimination,' said Aunt Judith in a reproving tone. The old ladies were very fond of boasting of their wealth and position, whereas, in reality, their nephew was the only barrier between them and the workhouse.

'Well, Aunt Judith,' replied Christian patiently, 'I will try and stay at home more in future. But you know it is time I was doing something to earn my own livelihood now. I cannot exist on your kindness all my life!'

He had learnt to humour these two silly old women. During the two years which had just passed he had gradually recognised the utter futility of endeavouring to make them realise the true state of their affairs. They spoke grandiloquently of the family solicitor : a man who had been in his grave for nearly a quarter of a century. It was simply impossible to instil into their minds any fact whatever, and such facts as had established themselves there were permanent. They belonged to another generation, and their mode of thought was a remnant of a forgotten and unsatisfactory period. To them Napoleon the First was a living man, Queen Victoria unheard of. The decay of their minds had been slow, and it had been Christian Vellacott's painful task to watch its steady progress. Day by day he had followed the gradual failing of each sense and power.

There is something pathetic about the decay of a mind which has been driven to death by constant work, but there is a compensating thought to alleviate the sadness. It may rattle and grow loose, like some worn-out engine, where the friction presses; but it will work till it collapses totally, and some of the work achieved is good and permanent. It is bound to be so. Infinitely sadder is the sight of a mind which is falling to pieces by reason of the rust that has eaten into its very core. For rust must needs mean idleness—and no human intellect *need* be idle. So it had been with these two old ladies. Born in a wofully unintellectual age they had never left a certain groove in life. When their brother married Christian Vellacott's grandmother, they had left his house in Honiton to go and live in Bodmin upon a limited but sufficient income. These 'sufficient incomes' are a curse: they do not allow of charity and make no call for labour.

When Christian Vellacott arrived in England, an orphan with no great wealth, he made it his first duty to visit the only living relations he possessed. He was just in time to save them, literally, from starvation. It was obvious that he could not make a literary livelihood in Bodmin, so he made a home for the two old wrecks of humanity in London. Their means, like their minds, were simply exhausted. Aunt Judith was ninety-three ; Aunt Hester ninety-one. During that vast blank (for blank it was, so far as their lives were concerned) stretching away back into a perspective of time which few around them could gauge—they had never been separated for one day. Like two apples they had grown side by side, until their very contact had engendered disease— a slow, deadly, creeping rot, finding its source at the point of contact, reaching its

goal at the heart of each. They had *existed*
thus with terrible longevity—lived a mere
animal life of sleeping and eating, such as
hundreds of women are living around us
now.

'Of course, you must learn to make your
daily bread, Nephew Vellacott!' answered
Aunt Hester. 'The desire does you credit;
but you should be careful into what society
you go without us. Girls are very design-
ing, and many a one would like to marry a
nephew of mine—eh, Judith?'

'Yes, that they would,' replied the old
lady. 'The minxes know that they might
do worse than catch the nephew of Judith
and Hester Vellacott!'

'Look at us,' continued Aunt Hester,
drawing up her shrunken old form with a
touch of pride. 'Look at us! We have

always avoided marriage, and we are very nice and happy, I am sure ! '

She waited for a confirmation of this bold statement, but Christian was not listening. He was leaning forward with his hands clasped between his knees, gazing into the fire. He was recalling the conversation which had passed in the little room in the Strand. Could he leave these two helpless old creatures? Could he get away from it all for a little time—away from the maddening prattle of unguided tongues, from the dread monotony of hopeless watching? He knew that he was wasting his manhood, neglecting his intellectual opportunities, and endangering his career; but his course of duty was marked out with terrible distinctness. He never saw the pathos of it, as a woman would have seen it, gathering perhaps some slight alleviation from the sight. It never entered his thoughts to complain, and he never conceived the idea of drawing comparisons between his position and that of other young men who, instead of being slaves to their relatives, made very good use of them. He merely went on doing his obvious duty and striving not to look forward too eagerly to a release at some future period.

Fortunately, Mrs. Strawd was not long in bringing in the simple evening meal; and the attention of the old ladies was at once turned to the mystery hidden beneath the dish-cover. What was it, and would there be enough for Nephew Vellacott?

Deftly, Christian poured out the tea. Two cups very weak and one stronger. Then two thin slices of crustless bread had to be buttered. This operation required great judgment and impartiality.

'Excuse me, Nephew Vellacott!' said Aunt Judith, with dangerous severity. 'Is that first slice intended for Aunt Hester? It appears to me that the butter is very thick —much thicker than on the second, which is doubtless intended for me!'

'Do you think so, Aunt Judith?' asked Christian in a voice purposely loud in order to drown Aunt Hester's remonstrance. 'Then I will take a little off!' He passed the knife harmlessly over the faulty slice, and laid the two side by side upon a plate. Then the old ladies promptly held a survey on them—that declared to be mor heavily buttered being awarded to Aunt Judith in recognition of her seniority.

With similar fruitful topics of conversation the meal was pleasantly despatched. The turn of Dick and Mick followed thereon. Dick, the property of Aunt Judith, was a canary of thoughtful temperament. The part he played in the domestic economy of the small household was a contemplative rather than an active one. Mick, Aunt Hester's bird, was of a more lively nature. He had, as a rule, something to say upon all subjects—and said it.

Now Aunt Hester, in her inmost heart, loved a silent bird, and secretly coveted Dick, but as Mick was her property, and Dick the silent was owned by Aunt Judith, she never lost an opportunity of enlarging upon the stupidity and uselessness of silent birds. Aunt Judith, on the other hand, admired a lively and talkative canary; consequently she was weighed down with the conviction that her sister's bird was the superior article. Altogether, birds as a topic of conversation were best avoided. Dick and Mick were housed in cages of similar build—indeed, most things were strictly in duplicate in the whole household. Every evening Christian brought the cages, and Aunt Judith and Aunt Hester carefully placed within the wires a small piece of bread-and-butter, which Nurse Strawd as carefully removed, untouched, the next morning.

When the birds' wants had been attended to, it was Christian's duty to settle the old ladies comfortably in their respective arm-chairs. This he did tenderly and cleverly as a woman, but it was not a pleasant sight to look upon. The man, with his lean strong face, long jaw, and prominent chin, was so obviously out of place. These peaceful duties were never meant for such as he. His some-what closely-set eyes were not such as wax tender over drowning flies, for even in repose they were somewhat direct and stern in their gaze. In fact, Christian Vellacott was so visibly created for strife and the forefront of life's battle, that it was almost painful to see him fulfilling a more peaceful avocation.

As a rule he devoted himself to the amusement of his aged relatives for an hour or so; but this evening he sat down to the piano at once, with the deliberate intention of playing them off to sleep. Ten o'clock was their hour for retiring, and before that they would not move, although they dozed in their chairs

He was no mean musician, this big West-countryman, with a true ear and a touch peculiarly light and tender for a man. He played gently and drowsily for some time, half forgetting that he was not alone in the room. Presently he turned round, letting his fingers rest on the keys. Aunt Judith was asleep, and Aunt Hester made a sign for him to go on playing. Five minutes more, gradually toned down till the very sounds seemed to fall asleep, and Aunt Hester was peacefully slumbering. Silently the player rose, and crossing the room, he resumed his seat at the table from which the white cloth had not yet been removed. Pen, ink, and paper were within reach, and in a few minutes he had written the following note :—

' Dear Sidney,

' May I retract the letter I wrote yesterday and accept your invitation? I have been requested to take a holiday, and, rather than offend the powers that be, have given in. I can think of no happier way of spending it than in seeing you all again and recalling the jolly old Prague days. With kind regards,

' Yours ever,

' Christian Vellacott.'

He folded the note and slipped it into an

envelope, which he addressed to 'Sidney Carew, Esq., St. Mary Western, Dorset.' Then he slipped noiselessly out of the room and upstairs to where Mrs. Strawd had a small sitting-room of her own. The little woman heard his footstep on the old creaking stairs, and opened the door of her room before he reached it.

'If I went away for three weeks,' he said, ' could you do without me?'

'Of course I could,' replied the little woman readily. 'Just you go away and take a holiday, Master Christian. You need it sorely, that I know. You do indeed. We shall get on splendidly without you. I'll just have my sister to come and stay, same as I did when you had to go to the Paris House of Parliament.'

'I have not had much of a holiday, you see, for two years now!'

'Of course you hav'n't, and you want it. It's only human nature—and you a young man that ought to be in the open air all day. For . an old woman like me it's different. We're made differently by the good God on purpose, I think !'

' Well, then, if your sister comes it must be understood, nurse, that I make the same arrangement with her as exists with you. She must simply be a duplicate of you—you understand ?'

The little woman laughed, lightly enough.

' Oh, yes, Master Christian, that is all right. But you need not have troubled about that. She never would have thought of such a thing as wages, I'm sure !'

' No,' replied he gravely, ' I know she would not, but it will be better, I think, to have it understood beforehand. Gratitude is a very nice thing to work for, but some work

is worth more than gratitude.   If you are
going out for your walk, perhaps you will
post this letter.'

Before Christian went to bed that night
he held a candle close to the mirror and
looked long and hard at his own reflection.
There were dark streaks under his eyes, his
small mouth was drawn and dry, his lips
colourless.   At each temple the bone stood
out rather prominently, and the skin was
brilliant in its whiteness and reflected the
light of the candle.   He felt his own pulse.
It was beating, at one moment fast and irregu-
lar, at the next it was hardly perceptible.

'Yes!' he muttered, with a professional
nod—in his training as a journalist he had
learnt a little of many sciences—'yes, old
Bodery was right.'

CHAPTER V

A RE-UNION

THE gentle August night had cooled and soothed the dusty atmosphere. All things looked fair, even in London. The placid Thames glided stealthily down to the sea, as if wishing to speed on unseen, to cast at last his reeking waters into the cool ocean. The bright brown sails, low hulls, and gaily painted spars of the barges dropping down with the stream added to the beauty of the scene.

Such was the morning that greeted Christian Vellacott, as he opened the door of his little Chelsea home and stepped forth a free man. When once he had made up his mind to go, every obstacle was thrown aside and his determination was now as great as had been his previous reluctance. He had no presentiment that he was taking an important step in life—one of those steps which we hardly notice at the time, but upon which we look back in after years and note how clear and definite it was, losing ourselves in vague conjecture as to what might have been had we held back.

Christian, being practical in all things, knew how to travel comfortably, dispensing with rugs and bags and such small packages as are understood to be dear to the elderly single female heart.

The smoky suburbs were soon left behind, and the smiling land gave forth such gentle, pastoral odours as only long confinement in cities can teach us to detect. Christian lowered the window, and the warm air played round him as it had not done for two long years.

The whizz of the wind past his face brought back the memory of the long, idle, happy days spent with his father in the Mediterranean, when they had been half sailors and wholly Bohemians, gliding from port to port, village to city, in their yacht, as free and careless as the wind. The warm breeze almost seemed to be coming to him from some parched Italian plain instead of pastoral Buckinghamshire.

Then his thoughts travelled still further back to his school-days in Prague, when his father and Mr. Carew were colleagues in a brilliant but unfortunate embassy. Five years had passed since then. The two fathers were now dead, and the children had dropped apart as men and women do when their own personal interests begin to engross them. Now again, in this late summer time, they were to meet. All, that is, who were left. The *débris*, as it were. Three voices there were whose tones would never more be heard in the round of merry jest. Mr. Carew, Walter Vellacott (Uncle Walter, the young ones called him), and little Charlie Carew, the bright-eyed sailor of the family, had all three travelled on. The two former, whose age and work achieved had softened their departure, were often spoken of with gently lowered voice, but little Charlie's name was never mentioned. It was a fatal mistake —this silence—if you will; but it was one of those mistakes which are often made in wisdom. In splendid solitary grandeur he lay awaiting the end of all things—the call of his Creator—in the grey ice-fields of the North. The darling of his ship, he had died with a smile in his blue eyes and a sad little jest upon his lips to cheer the rough fur-clad giants kneeling at his side. Time, the merciful, had healed, as best he could (which is by no means perfectly), the wound in the younger hearts. It is only the old that are quite beyond his powers ; he cannot touch them. Mrs. Carew, a woman with a patient face and a ready smile, was the only representative of the vanishing generation. Her daughters— ay! and perhaps her sons as well (though boys are not credited with so much tender divination)—knew the meaning of the little droop at the side of their mother's smiling lips. They detected the insincerity of her kindly laugh.

Shortly after leaving Exeter, Christian's station was reached. This was an old-fashioned seaport town, whose good fortune it was to lie too far west for a London watering-place, and too far east for Plymouth or Bristol. Sidney Carew was on the platform —a sturdy, typical Englishman, with a certain sure slowness of movement handed down to him by seafaring ancestors. The two friends had not met for many years, but with men absence has little effect upon affection. During the space of many years they may never meet and seldom write, but at the end that gulf of time is bridged over by a simple 'Halloa, old fellow!' and a warm grip. Slowly, piece by piece, the history of the past years comes out. Both are probably changed in thought and nature, but the old individuality remains, the old bond of friendship survives.

'Well, Sidney?'

'How are you?'

Simultaneously—and that was all. The changes were there in both, and noted by both, but not commented upon.

'Molly is outside with the dog-cart,' said Sidney; 'is your luggage forward?'

'Yes, that is it being pitched out now.'

It was with womanly foresight that Miss Molly Carew had elected to wait outside with the dog-cart while her brother met Christian on the platform. She feared a little natural embarrassment at meeting the old playfellow of the family, and concluded that the first moments would be more easily tided over here than at the train. Her fears were, as it turned out, unnecessary, but she did not know what Christian might be like after the lapse of years. Of herself she was sure enough, being one of those happy people who have no self-consciousness whatever.

On seeing her, Christian came forward at once, raising his hat and shaking hands as if they had parted the day before.

She saw at once that it was all right. This was Christian Vellacott as she had remembered him. She looked down at him as he stood with one hand resting on the splashboard, and he, looking up to her, smiled in return.

'Christian,' she said, 'do you know, I should scarcely have recognised you. You are so big, and—and you look positively ghastly!' She finished her remark with a little laugh which took away from the spoken meaning of it.

'Ghastly?' he replied. 'Thanks; I do not feel like it—only hungry. Hungry, and desperately glad to see a face which does not look overworked.'

'Meaning me?'

'Meaning you.'

She gave a little sarcastic nod, and pursed up a pair of very red lips.

'Nevertheless I am the only person in the house who does any work at all. Hilda, for instance——'

At this moment Sidney came up and interrupted them.

'Jump up in front, Chris,' he said; 'Molly will drive, while I sit behind. Your luggage will follow in the cart.'

The drive of six miles passed away very pleasantly. Molly's strong little hands were quite accustomed to the reins, and the men were free to talk, which, however, she found time to do as well. The two young people on the front seat stole occasional sidelong glances at each other. The clever mischievous little girl of Christian's recollection was transformed by the kindly hand of time into a fascinating and capable young lady. The uncertain profile had grown clear and regular. The truant hair was somewhat more under control, which, however, was all that could be said upon that subject. Only her eyes were unchanged, the laughing fearless eyes of old. Fearless they had been in the times of childish mischief and adventure; fearless they remained in face of life's graver mischances now.

Christian had been a shy and commonplace-enough boy as she recollected him. Now she found a self-possessed man of the world. Tall and strong of body she saw he was, and she felt that he possessed another strength—a strength of mind and will which, reaching out, can grasp and hold anything or everything.

With practised skill, Molly turned into the narrow gateway at a swinging trot, and then only was the house visible—a low, rambling building of brick and stone uncouthly mixed. Its chief outward characteristic was a promise of inward comfort. The sturdy manner in which its windows faced the scantily-wooded tableland that stretched away unbroken by

wall or hedgerow to the sea, implied a certain thickness of wall and woodwork. The
doorway which looked inland was singularly
broad, and bore signs about its stonework of
having once been even broader. The house
had originally been a hollow square, with a
roofless courtyard in the centre, into which
the sheep and cattle were in olden times
driven for safety at night against French
marauders. This had later on been roofed
in, and transformed into a roomy and comfortable hall, such as might be used as a
sitting-room. All around the house, except,
indeed, upon the seaward side, stood gnarled
and twisted trees; Scotch firs in abundance,
here and there a Weymouth pine, and occasionally a knotted dwarf oak with a tendency
to run inland. The garden was, however,
rich enough in shrubs and undergrowth, and
to the landward side was a gleam of still water,

being all that remained of a broad deep moat.

Mrs. Carew welcomed Christian at the open door. She said very little, but her manner was sufficiently warm and friendly to dispense with words.

'Where is Hilda?' asked Molly, as she leapt lightly to the ground.

'I do not know, dear. She is out, some-where; in the garden, I expect. You are before your time a little. The train must have been punctual, for a wonder. Had Hilda known, she would have been here to welcome you, I know, Christian.'

'I expect she is at the moat,' said Molly. 'Come along, Christian; we will go and look for her. This way.'

In the meantime Sidney had driven the dog-cart round to the stables, kneeling awk-wardly upon the back seat.

As Christian followed his fair guide down the little path leading to the moat, he began to feel that it was not so difficult after all to throw off the dull weight of anxiety that lay upon his mind. The thoughts about the 'Beacon' were after all not so very absorbing. The anxiety regarding the welfare of the two old ladies was already alleviated by distance. The strong sea air, the change to pleasant and kindly society, were already beginning their work.

Suddenly Molly stopped, and Christian saw that she was standing at the edge of a long still sheet of water bounded by solid stone-work, which, however, was crumbling away in parts, while everywhere the green moss grew in velvety profusion.

'Oh, Christian,' said Molly lightly, 'I suppose Sidney told you a little of our news. Men's letters are not discursive as a rule I know, but no doubt he told you—something.'

He was standing beside her at the edge of the moat, looking down into the deep clear water.

'Yes,' he replied slowly, 'yes, Molly; he told me a little in a scrappy, unsatisfactory way.'

A pained expression came into her eyes for a moment, and then she spoke, rather more quickly than was habitual with her, but without raising her voice.

'He told you—nothing about Hilda?' she said interrogatively.

He turned and looked down at her.

'No—nothing.'

Then he followed the direction of her eyes, and saw approaching them a young man and a maiden whose footsteps had been inaudible upon the moss-grown path. The man was of medium height, with an honest brown face. He was dressed for riding, and walked with a slight swagger, which arose less from conceit than from excessive riding on horseback. The maiden was tall and stately, and in her walk there was an old-fashioned grace of movement which harmonised perfectly with the old-world surroundings. She was looking down, and Christian could not see her face; but as she wore no hat, he saw and recognised her hair. This was of gold—not red, not auburn, not flaxen, but pure and living gold. The sun glinting through the trees shone upon it and gleamed, but in reality the hair gleamed without the aid of sunlight.

CHAPTER VI

BROKEN THREADS

THEY came forward, and suddenly the girl
raised her face.   She made a little hesitating movement of non-recognition, and
then suddenly her face was transformed by
a very pleasant smile.   There was something
peculiar in Hilda Carew's smile, which came
from the fact that her eyelashes were golden,
while her eyes were dark blue.   The effect
suggested a fascinating kitten.   In repose
her face was almost severe in its refined
beauty, and the set of her lips indicated a
certain self-reliance which with years might

become more prominent if trouble should arrive.

'Christian!' she exclaimed, 'I am sorry I did not know you.' They shook hands, and Molly hastened to introduce her sister's companion.

'Mr. Farrar,' she said; 'Mr. Vellacott.'

The two men shook hands, and Christian was disappointed. The grip of Farrar's fingers was limp and almost nerveless, in striking contradiction to the promise of his honest face and well-set person.

'Tea is ready,' said Molly somewhat hastily, 'let us go in.'

Hilda and her companion passed on in front, while Molly and Christian followed them. The latter purposely lagged behind, and his companion found herself compelled to wait for him.

'Look at the effect of the sunlight through

the trees upon that water,' said he, in a conversational way; ' it is quite green, and almost transparent.'

' Yes,' replied Molly, moving away tentatively, ' we see most peculiar effects over the moat. The water is so very still and deep.'

He raised his quiet eyes to her face, upon which the ready smile still lingered. As she met his gaze she raised her hand and pushed back a few truant wisps of hair which, curling forward like tendrils, tickled her cheek. It was a movement he soon learned to know.

' Yes,' he said absently. He was wondering in an analytical way whether the action was habitual with her, or significant of embarrassment. At length he turned to follow her, but Molly had failed in her object; the others had passed out of earshot.

' Tell me,' said Christian in a lowered voice, ' who is he ? '

' He is the squire of St. Mary Eastern, six miles from here,' she replied ; ' very well off ; very good to his mother, and in every way nice.'

Christian tore off a small branch which would have touched his forehead had he walked on without stooping. He broke it into small pieces, and continued throwing up at intervals into the air a tiny stick, hitting it with his hand as they walked on.

' And,' he said suggestively, ' and —— '

' Yes, Christian,' she replied decisively, ' they are engaged. Come, let us hurry ; I always pour out the tea. I told you before, if you remember, that I was the only person in the house who did any work.'

When Christian opened his eyes the

following morning, the soft hum of insects fell on his ear instead of the roar of London traffic. Through the open window the southern air blew upon his face. Above the sound of busy wings the distant sea sang its low dirge. It was a living perspective of sound. The least rustle near at hand overpowered it, and yet it was always there—an unceasing throb to be felt as much as heard. Some acoustic formation of the land carried the noise, for the sea was eight miles away. It was very peaceful ; for utter stillness is not peace. A room wherein an old clock ticks is infinitely more soothing than a noiseless chamber.

Nevertheless the feeling that forced itself into Christian Vellacott's waking thoughts was not peaceful. It was a sense of discomfort. Town-people expect too much from the country—that is the truth of it. They quite overlook the fact that where human beings are there can be no peace.

This sudden sense of restlessness annoyed him. He knew it so well. It had hovered over his waking head almost daily during the last two years, and here, in the depths of the country, he had expected to be without it. Moreover, he was conscious that he had not brought the cause with him. He had found it, waiting.

There were many things—indeed there was almost everything—to make his life happy and pleasant at St. Mary Western. But in his mind, as he woke up on this first morning, none of these things found place. He came to his senses thinking of the one little item which could be described as untoward—thinking of Hilda, and Hilda engaged to be married to Fred Farrar. It was not that he was in love with Hilda Carew himself. He had scarcely remembered her existence during the last two years. But this engagement jarred, and Farrar jarred. It was something more than the very natural shock which comes with the news that a companion of our youth is about to be married—a shock which seems to shake the memory of that youth ; to confuse the background of our life. It is by means of such shocks as these that Fate endeavours vainly to make us realise that the past is irrevocable —that we are passing on, and that that which has been can never be again. And at the same time we learn something else : namely, that the past is not by any means unchangeable. So potential is To-day that it not only holds To-morrow in the hollow of its hand, but it can alter Yesterday.

Christian Vellacott lay upon his bed in unwonted idleness, gazing vaguely at the flying clouds. The window was open, and the song of the distant sea rose and fell with a rhythm full of peace. But in this man's mind there was no peace. In all probability there never would be complete peace there, because Ambition had set its hold upon him. He wanted to do more than there was time for. Like many of us, he began by thinking that Life is longer than it is. Its whole length is in those ' long, long thoughts ' of Youth. When those are left behind, we settle down to work, and the rest of the story is nothing but labour. Vellacott resented this engagement because he felt that Hilda Carew had stepped out of that picture which formed what was probably destined to be the happiest time of his life— his Youth. For the unhappiness of Youth is preferable to the resignation of Age. He felt that she had willingly resigned something which he would on no account have given up.

Above all, he felt that it was a mistake. This was, of course, at the bottom of it. He probably felt that it was a pity. We usually feel so on hearing that a pretty and charming girl is engaged to be married. We think that she might have done so much better for herself, and we grow pensive or possibly sentimental over her lost opportunity when contemplating him in the mirror as he shaves. Like all so-called happy events, an engagement is not usually a matter of universal rejoicing. Someone is, in all probability, left to think twice about it. But Christian Vellacott was not prepared to admit that he was in that position.

He was naturally of an observant habit —his father had been one of the keenest-sighted men of his day—and he had graduated at the subtlest school in the world. He unwittingly fell to studying his fellow-men whenever the opportunity presented itself, and the result of this habit was a certain classification of detail. He picked up little scraps of evidence here and there, and these were methodically pigeon-holed away, as a lawyer stores up the correspondence of his clients.

With regard to Frederick Farrar, Vellacott had only made one note. The squire of St. Mary Eastern was apparently very similar to his fellows. He was an ordinary young British squire with a knowledge of horses and a highly-developed fancy for smart riding-breeches and long boots. He had probably received a fair education, but this had ceased when he closed his last school-book. The seeds of knowledge had been sown, but they lacked moisture and had failed to grow. He was good-natured, plucky in a hard-headed British way, and gentlemanly.

In all this there was nothing exceptional—
nothing to take note of—and Vellacott only
remembered the limpness of Frederick
Farrar's grasp. He thought of this too
persistently and magnified it. And this being
the only mental note made, was rather hard
on the young squire of St. Mary Eastern.

Vellacott thought of these things while
he dressed, he thought of them intermittently
during the unsettled, noisy, country breakfast, and when he found himself walking
beside the moat with Hilda later on he was
still thinking of them.

They had not yet gathered into their
hands the threads which had been broken
years before. At times they hit upon a
topic of some slight common interest, but
something hovered in the air between them.
Hilda was gay, as she had always been, in
a gentle, almost purring way; but a certain

constrained silence made itself felt at times, and they were both intensely conscious of it.

Vellacott was fully aware that there was something to be got over, and so instead of skipping round it, as a woman might have done, he went blundering on to the top of it.

'Hilda,' he said suddenly, 'I have never congratulated you.'

She bent her head in a grave little bow which was not quite English; but she said nothing.

'I can only wish you all happiness,' he continued rather vaguely.

Again she made that mystic little motion of the head, but did not look towards him, and never offered the assistance of smile or word.

'A long life, a happy one, and your own

will,' he added more lightly, looking down into the green water of the moat.

'Thank you,' she said, standing quite still beside him.

And then there followed an awkward pause. It was Vellacott who finally broke the silence in the only way left to him.

'I like Farrar,' he said. 'I am sure he will make you happy. He—is a lucky fellow.'

At the end of the walk that ran the whole length of that part of the moat which had been allowed to remain intact, she made a little movement as if to turn aside beneath the hazel trees and towards the house. But he would not let her go. He turned deliberately upon his heel and waited for her. There was nothing else to do but acquiesce. They retraced their steps with that slow reflectiveness which comes when one walks backwards and forwards over the same ground.

There is something eminently conversational in the practice of walking to and fro. For that purpose it is better than an arm-chair and a pipe, or a piece of knitting.

Occasionally Vellacott dropped a pace behind, apparently with a purpose; for when he did so he raised his eyes instantly. He seemed to be slowly detailing the maiden, and he frowned a little. She was exactly what she had promised to be. The singularly golden hair which he had last seen flowing freely over her slight young shoulders had acquired a decorousness of curve, although the hue was unchanged. The shoulders were exactly the same in contour, on a slightly larger scale; and the manner of carrying her head—a manner peculiarly her own, and suggestive of a certain gentle wilfulness—was unaltered.

And yet there was a change : that subtle change which seems to come to girls suddenly, in the space of a week—of one night. And this man was watching her with his analytical eyes, wondering what the change might be.

He was more or less a bookworm, and he possibly thought that this subject—this pleasant young subject walking beside him in a blue cotton dress—was one which might easily be grasped and understood if only one gave one's mind to it. Hence the little frown. It denoted the gift of his mind. It was the frown that settled over his eyes when he cut the pages of a deep book and glanced at the point of his pencil.

He had read many books, and he knew a number of things. But there is one subject of which very little can be learnt in books—

precisely the subject that walked in a blue
cotton dress by Christian Vellacott's side at
the edge of the moat. If anyone thinks that
book-learning can aid this study, let him read
the ignorance of Gibbon, comparing it with
the learning of that cheery old ignoramus
Montaigne. And Vellacott was nearer to
Gibbon in his learning than to Montaigne
in his careless ignorance of those things that
are written in books.

He glanced at her; he frowned and
brought his whole attention to bear upon her,
and he could not even find out whether she
was pleased to listen to his congratulations,
or angry, or merely indifferent. It was rather
a humiliating position for a clever man—for
a critic who knew himself to be capable of
understanding most things, of catching the
drift of most thoughts, however imperfectly
expressed. He was vaguely conscious of

defeat. He felt that he was nonplussed by a pair of soft round eyes like the eyes of a kitten, and the dignified repose of a pair of demure red lips. Both eyes and lips, as well as shoulders and golden hair, were strangely familiar and strangely strange by turns.

With one finger he twisted the left side of his moustache into his mouth, and, dragging at it with his teeth, distorted his face in an unbecoming if reflective manner, which was habitually indicative of the deepest attention.

While reflecting, he forgot to be conversational, and Hilda seemed to be content with silence. So they walked the length of the moat twice without speaking, and might have accomplished it a third time, had little Stanley Carew not appeared upon the scene with the impulsive energy of his thirteen years, begging Christian to bowl him some really swift overhands.

CHAPTER VII

PUPPETS

'AH! It goes. It goes already!'

The speaker—the Citizen Morot—slowly rubbed his white hands one over the other.

He was standing at the window of a small house in an insignificant street on the southern side of the Seine. He was remarkably calm —quite the calmest man within the radius of a mile; for the insignificant little street was in an uproar. There was a barricade at each end of it. Such a barricade as Parisians love. It was composed of a few overturned omnibuses; for the true Parisian is a cynic. He likes overturned things, and he loves to see objects of peace converted to purposes of war. He is not content that ploughshares be beaten into swords. He prefers altar-rails. And so this little street was blocked at either end by a barricade of overturned omnibuses, of old hampers and empty boxes, of a few loads of second-hand bricks and paving-stones brought from the scene of some drainage operations round the corner.

In the street between the barricades, surged, hooted, and yelled that wildest and most dangerous of incomprehensibles — a Paris mob. Half a dozen orators were speaking at once, and no one was listening to them. Here and there amidst the rabble a voice was raised at times with suspicious persistence.

'*Vive le Roi!*' it cried. 'Long live the King!'

A few took up the refrain, but the general tone was negative. It was not so much a question of upholding anything as of throwing down that which was already up.

'Down with the Republic!' was the favourite cry. 'Down with the President! Down with everything!'

And each man cried down his favourite enemy.

The Citizen Morot listened, and his contemptuous mouth was twisted with a delicate, subtle smile.

'Ah!' he muttered. 'The voice of the people. The howling of the wolves. Go on, go on, my braves. Cry "Long live the King," and soon you will begin to believe that you mean it. They are barking now. Let them bark. Soon we shall teach them to bite, and then—then, who knows?'

His voice dropped almost to a whisper, and he stood there amidst the din and hubbub —dreaming. At last he raised his hand to his forehead—a prominent rounded forehead, flat as the palm of one's hand from eyebrow to eyebrow, and curving at either side, sharply, back to deep-sunken temples.

'Ah!' he exclaimed, with a little laugh ; and he drew from an inner pocket a delicately scented pocket-handkerchief, with which he wiped his brow. 'If I get excited now, what will it be when they begin—to bite?'

All this while the orators were shouting their loudest, and the voices dispersed throughout the crowd raised at intervals their short sharp cry of—

'Long live the King!'

And the police? There were only two agents attached to the immediate neighbourhood, and they were smoking cigars and drinking absinthe in two separate cellars, with the door locked on the outside. They were prisoners of war of the most resigned type. The room in which stood the Citizen Morot was dark, and wisely so. For the Parisian street politician can make very pretty practice of a lighted petroleum-lamp with an empty bottle or half a brick. The window was wide open, and the wooden shutters were hooked back.

The attitude of the man was interested and slightly self-satisfied. It suggested that of the manager of a theatre looking down from an upper-tier box upon a full house and a faultless stage. At the same time he was keeping what sailors call a very ' bright lookout' towards either end of the street. From his elevated position he was able to see over the barricades, and he watched with intense interest the movements of two women (or perhaps men disguised as such) who stood in the centre of the street just beyond each obstruction.

There was something dramatic in the motionless attitude of these two women, standing guard alone in the deserted street, on the wrong side of the barricades.

At times Morot leant well out of the window and listened. Then he stood back again and contemplated the crowd.

Each orator was illuminated by a naphtha 'flare,' which, being held in unsteady hands, flickered and wavered, casting strange gleams of light over the evil faces upturned towards it. At times one speaker would succeed in raising a laugh or extracting a groan, and when he did so those listening to his rivals turned and surged towards him. There was plenty of movement. It was what the newspapers call an animated scene—or a disgraceful scene—according to their political bias.

The Citizen Morot could not hear the jokes nor distinguish the cause of the groaning. But he did not seem to mind much. The speeches were not of the description to ·be given in full in the morning papers. There were, fortunately, no reporters present. It was the frank eloquence of the slaughter-house—the unclad humour of the market.

Suddenly one of the women—she who was posted at the southern end of the street —raised both her arms, and the Citizen leant far out of the window. He was very eager, and his hawk-like eyes blinked perpetually. His hand was raised to his mouth, and the lights of the orators gleamed on something that he held in his fingers—something that looked like silver.

The woman held her two arms straight up into the air for some moments, then she suddenly crossed them twice, turning at the same moment and scrambling over the barricade. A long shrill whistle rang out over the heads of the mob, and its effect was almost instantaneous. The 'flares' disappeared like magic. Dark figures swarmed up the lamp-posts and extinguished the feeble lights. The voice of the orator was still. Silence and darkness reigned over that insignificant little street on the southern side of the Seine. Then came the clatter of cavalry—the rattle of horses' feet, and the ominous clank of empty scabbards against spur and buckle. A word of command, and a scrambling halt. Then silence again, broken only by the shuffling of feet (not too well clad) in the darkness between the barricades.

The Citizen Morot leant recklessly out of the window, peering into the gloom. He forgot to make use of the delicately scented pocket-handkerchief now, and the drops of perspiration trickled slowly down his face.

The soldiers shuffled in their saddles. Some of the spirited little Arabs pawed the pavement. One of them squealed angrily, and there was a slight commotion somewhere in the rear ranks—an equine difference of opinion. The officers had come forward to the barricade and were consulting together. The question was—what was there behind that barricade? It might be nothing—it might be everything. In Paris one can never tell. At last one of them determined to see for himself. He scrambled up, putting his foot through the window of an omnibus in passing. Against the dim light of the street-lamp beyond, his slight, straight figure stood out in bold relief. It was a splendid mark for a man with chalked sights to his rifle.

' Ah ! ' muttered the Citizen, ' you are all right this time—master, the young officer.

They are only barking. Next time perhaps it will be quite another history.'

The officer turned and disappeared. After the lapse of a few moments a dozen words of command were shouted, and upon them followed the sharp click of hilt on scabbard as the sabres fell home.

After a pause it became evident that the barricade was being destroyed. And then lights flashed here and there. In a compact column the cavalry advanced at a trot. The street was empty.

Citizen Morot turned away and sat down on a chair that happened to be placed near the window. His finely-drawn eyebrows were raised with a questioning weariness.

'Pretty work!' he ejaculated. 'Pretty work for—my father's son! So grand, so open, so noble!'

He waited there, in the darkness, until

the cavalry had been withdrawn and the local firemen were at work upon the barricade. Then, when order was fully restored, he left the house, walking quietly down the length of the insignificant little street.

Ten minutes later he entered the tobacco-shop in the Rue St. Gingolphe. Mr. Jacquetot was at his post, behind the counter near the window, with the little tin box containing postage-stamps in front of him upon his desk. He was always there—like the poor. He laid aside the ' Petit Journal ' and wished the new-comer a courteous, though breathless, good-evening.

The salutation was returned gravely and pleasantly. The Citizen Morot lingered a moment and remarked that it was a warm evening. He never seemed to be in a hurry. Then he passed on into the little room behind the shop.

There he found Lerac, the foreman of the slaughter-house. The butcher was pale with excitement. His rough clothing was dishevelled; his stringy black hair stood up uncouthly in the centre of his head, while over his temples it was plastered down with perspiration and suet pleasingly mingled.

'Well?' he exclaimed with triumphant interrogation.

'Good,' said Morot. 'Very good. It marches, my friend. It marches already.'

'Ah! But you are right. The People see you—it is a power!'

'It is,' acquiesced Morot fervently.

How he hated this man!

'And you stayed to the last?' inquired Lerac. He was rather white about the lips for a brave man.

'Till the last,' echoed Morot, taking up

some letters addressed to him which lay on the table.

'And the street was quite clear before they broke through the barrier?'

'Quite—the People did not wait.' He seemed to resign himself to conversation, for he put the letters into his pocket and sat down. 'Had you,' he inquired, 'any difficulty in getting them away?'

'Oh no,' somewhat loftily and quite unsuspicious of irony. 'The passages were narrow, of course; but we had allowed for that in our organisation. Organisation and the People, see you——'

'Yes,' replied Morot. 'Organisation and the People.' Like Lerac, he stopped short, apparently lost in the contemplation of the vast possibilities presented to his mental vision by the mere thought of such a combination.

'Well!' exclaimed the butcher energetically, 'I must move on. I have meetings. I merely wished to hear from you that all was right—that no one was caught.'

He was bubbling over with excitement and the sense of his own huge importance.

The Citizen Morot raised his secretive eyes.

'Good-night,' he said, with an insolence far too fine for the butcher's comprehension.

'Well—good-night. We may congratulate ourselves, I think, Citizen!'

'I congratulate you,' said Morot. 'Good-night.'

'Good-night.'

It is probable that, had Lerac looked back, there would have been murder done in the small room behind the tobacco-shop. But the contemptuous smile soon vanished from the face of the Citizen Morot. No smile lingered there long. It was not built upon smiling lines at all.

Then he took up his letters. There were only two of them : one bearing the postmark of a small town in Morbihan, the other hailing from England.

He replaced the first in his pocket unread ; the second he opened. It was written in French.

'There are difficulties,' it said. 'Can you come to me? Cross from Cherbourg to Southampton—train from thence to this place, and ask for Signor Bruno, an Italian refugee, living at the house of Mrs. Potter, a *ci-devant* laundress.'

The Citizen Morot rubbed his chin thoughtfully with the back of his hand, making a sharp, grating sound.

'That old man,' he said, 'is getting past his work. He is losing nerve ; and nerve is a thing that we cannot afford to lose.'

Then he turned to the letter again.

'Ah!' he exclaimed suddenly; 'St. Mary Western. He is there—how very strange. What a singular coincidence!'

He fell into a reverie with the letter before him.

'Carew is dead—but still I can manage it. Perhaps it is just as well that he is dead. I was always afraid of Carew.'

Then he wrote a letter, which he addressed to Signor Bruno, care of Mrs. Potter, St. Mary Western, Dorset.'

'I shall come,' he wrote, 'but not in the way you suggest. I have a better plan. You must not know me when we meet.'

He purchased a twenty-five centime stamp from Mr. Jacquetot, and posted the letter with his own hand in the little wall-box at the corner of the Rue St. Gingolphe.

CHAPTER VIII

FALSE METAL

THERE was, however, no cricket for Stanley Carew that morning. When they came within sight of the house Mrs. Carew emerged from an open window carrying several letters in her hand. She was not hurrying, but walking leisurely, reading a letter as she walked.

'Just think, Hilda dear,' she said, with as much surprise as she ever allowed herself. 'I have had a letter from the Vicomte d'Audierne. You remember him?'

'Yes,' said the girl; 'I remember him, of course. He is not the sort of man one forgets.'

'I always liked the Viscount,' said Mrs. Carew, pensively looking at the letter she held in her hand. 'He was a good friend to us at one time. I never understood him, and I like men whom one does not understand.'

Hilda laughed.

'Yes,' she answered vaguely.

'Your father admired him tremendously,' Mrs. Carew went on to say. 'He said that he was one of the cleverest men in France, but that he had fallen in a wrong season, and would not adapt himself. Had France been a monarchy, the Vicomte d'Audierne would have been in a very different position.'

Vellacott did not open his own letters. He seemed to be interested in the conversation of these ladies. He was not a reserved man, but a secretive, which is quite a different thing. Reserve is natural—it comes unbidden, and often unwelcome. Secretiveness is born of circumstances. Some men find it imperative to cultivate it, although their soul revolts within them. In professional or social matters it is often merely an expediency—in some cases it almost feels like a crime. There are some secrets which cannot be divulged; there are some deceptions which a certain book-keeper will record upon the credit side of our account.

Like most young men who have got on in their calling, Christian Vellacott held his career in great respect. He felt that any sacrifice made for it carried its own reward. He thought that it levelled scruples and justified deceptions.

He knew this Vicomte d'Audierne by reputation; he wished to hear more of him; and so he feigned ignorance—listening.

'What has he written about?' inquired Hilda.

'To ask if he may come and see us. I suppose he means to come and stay.'

Vellacott looked what the French call 'contraried.'

'When?' asked the girl.

'On Monday week.'

And then Mrs. Carew turned to her other letters. Vellacott took the budget addressed to him, and walked away to where an iron table and some chairs stood in the shade of a deodar.

In a few minutes he looked still more put out. He had learnt of the disturbances in Paris, and was reading a rather panic-stricken letter from Mr. Bodery. The truth was that there was no one in the office of the 'Beacon' who knew anything whatever about French home politics but Christian Vellacott.

A continuance of these disturbances would necessarily assume political importance, and might even lead to a crisis. This meant an instant recall for Vellacott. In a crisis his presence in London or Paris was absolutely necessary to the 'Beacon.'

His holiday had barely lasted twenty-four hours, and there was already a question of recall. It happened also that within that short space a considerable change had come over Vellacott. The subtle influence of a country life and possibly the low peaceful song of the distant sea were already beginning to make themselves felt. He actually detected a desire to sit still and do nothing—a feeling of which he had not hitherto been conscious. He was distinctly averse to leaving St. Mary Western just yet. But there is one task-master who knows no mercy and makes no allowances. Some of us who serve him know it to our cost, and yet we would be content to serve no other. That taskmaster is the Public.

Vellacott was a public servant, and he knew his position.

Somewhat later in the morning Molly and Hilda found him still seated at the table, writing with that concentrated rapidity which only comes with practice.

'I am sorry,' he said, looking up, 'but I must send off a telegram. I shall walk in to the station.'

'I was just coming,' said Hilda, 'to ask if you would drive me in. I want to get some things.'

'And,' added Molly, 'there are some domestic commissions—butcher, baker, &c.'

Vellacott expressed his entire satisfaction with the arrangement, and by the time he had finished his letter the dog-cart was waiting at the door.

Several of the family were standing round the vehicle talking in a desultory manner, and Vellacott learnt then for the first time that Frederick Farrar had left home that same morning to attend a midland race-meeting.

It was one of those brilliant summer days when it is quite impossible to be pessimistic and exceedingly difficult to compass pre-occupation. The light breeze bowling over the upland from the sea had just sufficient strength to blow away all mental cobwebs. Also, Christian Vellacott had suddenly given way to one of those feelings which sometimes come to us without apparent reason. The present was joyous enough without the aid of the ever-to-be-bright future, and Vellacott felt that, after all, French politics and Frederick Farrar did not quite monopolise the world.

Hilda was on this occasion more talkative

than usual. There was in her manner a new sense of ease, almost of familiarity, which Vellacott could not understand. He noticed that she spoke invariably in generalities, avoiding all personal matters. Of herself she said no word, though she appeared willing enough to answer any question he might ask. She led him on to talk of himself and his work, listening gravely to his account of the little household at Chelsea. He made the best of this topic, and even treated it in a merry vein; but her smile, though sincere enough, was of short duration and not in itself encouraging. She appeared to see the pathos of it instead of the humour. Suddenly, in the middle of a particularly funny story about Aunt Judith, she interrupted him and changed the conversation entirely. She did not again refer to his home life.

As they were returning in the full glare

of the mid-day sun, they descried in front of
them the figure of an old man ; he was walking painfully and making poor progress.
Carefully dressed in black broadcloth, he
wore a soft felt hat of a shape seldom seen in
England.

'I believe,' said Hilda, as they approached
him, 'that is Signor Bruno. Yes, it is. Please
pull up, Christian. We must give him a
lift !'

Christian obeyed her. He thought he
detected a shade of annoyance in Hilda's
voice, with which he fully sympathised.

On hearing the sound of the wheels, the
old man looked up in surprise, as a deaf
person might have been expected to do.
This movement showed a most charming old
face, surrounded by a halo of white hair and
beard. The features were almost perfect,
and might in former days have been a trifle

cold, by reason of their perfection. Now, however, they were softened by the touch of years, and Signor Bruno was the living semblance of guilelessness and benevolence.

'How do you do, Signor Bruno?' said Hilda, speaking rather loudly and very distinctly. 'You are back from London sooner than you expected, are you not?'

'Ah! my dear young lady,' he replied, courteously removing his hat and standing bareheaded. 'Ah! now indeed the sun shines upon me. Yes, I am back from London—a most terrible place—terrible— terrible—terrible! As I walked along just now I said to myself: " The sun is warm, the skies are blue; yonder is the laughing sea, and yet, Bruno, you sigh for Italy." This is Italy, Miss Hilda—Italy with a northern fairy walking in it!'

Hilda smiled her quick surprising smile,

and hastened to speak before the old gentleman recovered his breath.

'Allow me to introduce to you Sidney's friend, Mr. Vellacott, Signor Bruno!'

Sidney's friend, Mr. Vellacott, was by this time behind her. He had alighted, and was employed in arranging the back seat of the dog-cart. When Signor Bruno looked towards him, he found Christian's eyes fixed upon his face with a quiet persistence which might have been embarrassing to a younger man. He raised his hat and murmured something unintelligible in reply to the Italian's extensive salutation.

'Sidney Carew's friends are, I trust, mine also!' said Signor Bruno, as he replaced his picturesque hat.

Christian smiled spasmodically and continued arranging the seat. He then came round to the front of the cart and made a sign to Hilda that she should move into the right-hand seat and drive. Signor Bruno saw the sign, and said urbanely:

'You will, if you please, resume your seat. I will place myself behind!'

'Oh, no! You must allow me to sit behind!' said Christian.

'But why, my dear sir? That would not be correct. You are Mr. Carew's guest, and I—I am only a poor old Italian runaway, who is accustomed to back seats; all my life I have occupied back seats, I think, Mr. Vell'cott. There is no reason why I should aspire to better things now!'

The old fellow's voice was strangely balanced between pathos and a peculiar self-abnegating humour.

'If we were both to take our hats off again, I think it would be easy to see why you should sit in front!' said Christian with

a laugh, which, although quite genial, somehow closed the discussion.

'Ah!' replied the old gentleman with
outspread hands. 'There you have worsted
me. After that I am silent, and—I obey!'

He climbed into the cart with a little
senile joke about the stiffness of his aged
limbs. He chattered on in his innocent,
childish way until the village was reached.
Here he was deposited on the dusty road at
the gate of a small yellow cottage where
he had two rooms. The seat was re-
arranged, and amidst a volley of thanks
and salutations, Hilda and Christian drove
away. Presently Hilda looked up and said :

'Is he not a dear old thing? I believe,
Christian, in all the various local information
I have given you, I have never told you
about Signor Bruno. I shall reserve him
for the next awkward pause that occurs.'

'Yes,' replied Christian quietly. 'He seems very nice.'

Something in his tone seemed to catch her attention. She half turned as if to hear more, but he said nothing. Then she raised her eyes to his face, which was not expressive of anything in particular.

'Christian,' she said gravely, 'you do not like him?'

Looked upon as a mere divination of thought, this was very quick; but he seemed in no way perturbed. He turned and looked down with a smile at her grave face.

'No,' he replied. 'Not very much.'

'Why?'

'I do not know. There is something wrong about him, I think!'

She laughed and shook her head.

'What do you mean?' she asked. 'How can there be anything wrong with him

—anything that would affect us, at all events?'

He shrugged his shoulders, still smiling.

'He says he is an Italian?'

'Yes,' she replied.

'I say he is a Frenchman,' said Christian, suddenly turning towards her. 'Italians do not talk English as he talks it.'

She looked puzzled.

'Do you know him?' she asked.

'No; not yet. I know his face. I have seen it or a photograph of it somewhere, and at some time. I cannot tell when or where yet, but it will come to me.'

'When it does come,' said Hilda, with a smile, 'you will find that it is someone else. I can assure you Signor Bruno is an Italian, and beyond that he is the nicest old gentleman imaginable.'

'Well,' replied Christian. 'In the meantime I vote that we do not trouble ourselves about him.'

The subject was dropped, and not again referred to until after they had reached home, when Hilda informed her mother that Signor Bruno had returned.

'Oh, indeed,' was the reply. 'I am very glad. You must ask him to dinner to-morrow evening. Is he not a nice old man, Christian?'

'Very,' replied Christian, almost before the words were out of her lips. 'Yes, very nice.' He looked across the table to-wards Hilda with an absolutely expression-less composure.

During the following day, which he passed with Sidney and Stanley at sea in a little cutter belonging to the Carews, Christian learnt, without asking many questions, all that Signor Bruno had vouchsafed in the way of information respecting himself. It was a short story and an old one, such as many a white-haired Italian could tell to-day. A life, income, and energy devoted to a cause which never had much promise of reward. Failure, exile, and a life closing in a land where the blue skies of Italy are known only by name, where Maraschino is at a premium, and long black cigars almost unobtainable.

Hilda was engaged on this day to lunch and spend the afternoon with Mrs. Farrar, at Farrar Court. Molly and Christian were to drive over for her in the evening. This programme was carried out, but the young people lingered rather longer at Farrar Court listening to the quaint old-world recollections of its white-haired hostess than was allowed for. Consequently they were late, and heard the first dinner-bell ringing as they drove up the lane that led in a casual way to their home. (This lane was characteristic of the house. It turned off unobtrusively from the high road at right angles with the evident intention of leading nowhere.) A race up-stairs ensued and a hurried toilet. Molly and Christian met on the stairs a few minutes later. Christian had won the race, for he was ready, while Molly struggled with a silver necklace that fitted closely round her throat. Of course he had to help her. While waiting patiently for him to master the intricacies of the old silver clasp, Molly said :

'Oh, Christian, there is one place you have not seen yet. Quite close at hand too.'

'Ye—es,' he replied absently, as he at length fixed the clasp. 'There, it is done !'

As he held open the drawing-room door, he said :

'What is the place I have to see ? '

Signor Bruno, who was seated at the far

end of the room with Mrs. Carew, rose as he heard the door opened, and advanced to meet Molly.

'Porton Abbey,' she said over her shoulder as she advanced into the room. 'You must see Porton Abbey.'

The Italian shook hands with the new-comers and made a clever, laughing reference to Christian's politeness of the previous day. At this moment Hilda entered, and as soon as she had returned Signor Bruno's courteous salutation Molly turned towards her.

'Hilda,' she said, 'we have never shown Christian Porton Abbey.'

'No,' was the reply. 'I have been re-serving it for some afternoon when we do not feel very energetic. Unfortunately, we cannot get inside the Abbey now, though.'

'Why?' asked Christian without looking towards Hilda. He had discovered that

Signor Bruno was attempting to keep up a conversation with his hostess, while he took in that which was passing at the other end of the room. The old man was seated, and his face was within the radius of light cast by a shaded lamp. Christian, who stood, was in the shade.

'Because it is a French monastery,' replied Molly. 'Here,' she added, 'is a flower for your coat, as you say the button-hole is warped by constant pinning in of stalks.'

'Thanks,' he replied, stooping a little in order that she could reach the button-hole of his coat. She was in front of him, directly between him and Signor Bruno; but he could see over her head. 'What sort of monastery is it?' he continued conversationally. 'I did not know that there were any establishments of that sort in England.'

Hilda looked up rather sharply from an illus-

trated newspaper she happened to be studying.
She knew that he was not adhering strictly to
the truth. From her point of vantage behind
the newspaper she continued to watch Christian, and she realised during the minutes that
followed, that this was indeed the brilliant
young journalist of whose fame Farrar had
spoken as already known in London.

Signor Bruno's conversation with Mrs.
Carew became at this moment somewhat
muddled.

'There, you see,' said Molly vivaciously,
'we endeavour to interest him by retailing
the simple annals of our neighbourhood, and
his highness simply disbelieves us!'

'Not at all,' Christian hastened to add,
with a laugh. 'It simply happened that I
was surprised. It shall not occur again.
But tell me, what short of monastery is it?
Dominican? Franciscan? Carmelite?——'

'Oh, goodness! I do not know.'

'Perhaps,' said Christian, advancing towards the Italian—'Perhaps Signor Bruno can tell us.'

'What is that, Mr. Vell'cott?' asked the old gentleman, making a movement as if about to raise his curved hand to his ear, but restraining himself upon second thoughts.

Hilda noticed that, instead of raising his voice, Christian spoke in the same tone, or even lower, as he said:

'We want some details of the establishment at Porton Abbey, Signor Bruno.'

The old gentleman made a little grimace expressive of disgust, at the same time spreading out his hands as if to ward off something hurtful.

'Ach!' he said, 'do not ask me. I know nothing of such people, and wish to learn no more. It is to them that my poor country owes her downfall. No, no; leave them alone. I always take care of myself against —against—what you say—*ces gens-là !* '

Christian awaited the answer in polite silence, and, when Signor Bruno had again turned to Mrs. Carew, he looked across the room towards Hilda with the same expression of vacant composure that she had noticed on a previous occasion. The accent with which Signor Bruno had spoken the few words of French was of the purest Parisian, entirely free from the harshness which an Italian rarely conquers.

After dinner Hilda went out of the open window into the garden alone. Christian, who had seated himself at a small table in the drawing-room, did not move. Sidney and his mother were talking with the Italian.

The young journalist was stooping over a book; a vase of flowers stood in front of him, but by the movement of his arm it appeared as if he were drawing instead of reading. Presently a faint low whistle came from the garden. Though soft, the sound was very clear, and each note distinctly given. It was like the beginning of a refrain which broke off suddenly and was repeated. Signor Bruno gave a little start and a quick upward glance.

'What is that?' he asked, with a little laugh, as if at the delicacy of his own nerves.

'Oh,' replied Mrs. Carew, 'the whistle, you mean. That is our family signal. The children were in the habit of calling each other by that means in bygone years. I expect they are in the garden now, and wish us to join them.'

Mrs. Carew knew that Molly was not in the garden, but in making this intentional mistake she showed the wisdom of her kind.

'It seems to me,' said Signor Bruno, 'that the air—the refrain, one might call it— is familiar.'

Christian Vellacott smiled suddenly behind his screen of flowers, but did not move or look up.

'I expect,' explained Sidney, 'that you have heard the air played upon the bugle. It is the French "retraite," played by the patrol in garrison towns at night.'

In the meantime Christian had cut the fly-leaf from the book before him, and, after carefully folding it, he placed the paper in his breast-pocket. Then he rose and passed out of the open window into the garden.

Immediately Signor Bruno asked his hostess a few polite questions regarding her guest—what was his occupation, how long he was going to stay, and whether she did not agree with him in considering that their young friend had a remarkably interesting face. In the course of his remarks the old gentleman rose and crossed to the table where Christian had been sitting. There was a flower there which he had not seen in England before. Absently he took up the book which Christian had just been studying, and very naturally turned to the title-page. The fly-leaf was gone! When he laid the volume down again he replaced it in the identical position in which he had found it.

CHAPTER IX

A CLUE

WHEN Christian left the drawing-room he walked quickly down the moss-grown path to the moat. Hilda was standing at the edge of the dark water, and as he joined her she turned and walked slowly by his side.

'You are a most unsatisfactory person,' she said gravely after a few moments.

He looked down at her without replying. His eyes softened for a moment into a smile, but his lips remained grave.

'You deliberately set yourself,' she continued, ' to shatter one illusion after another.

You have made me feel quite old and worldly to-night, and the worst of it is that you are invariably right. It is most annoying.'

Her voice was only half-playful. There was a shade of sadness in it. Christian must have divined her thoughts, for he said :

'Do not let us quarrel over Signor Bruno. I dare say I am wrong altogether.'

She looked slowly round. Her eyes rested on the dark surface of the water, where the shadows lay deep and still; then she raised them to the trees, clearly outlined against the sky.

'I suppose that such practical matter-of-fact people as you are proof against mere outward influences.'

'So I used to imagine, but I am beginning to find that outward things are very important after all. In London it seemed only natural that everyone should live in a hurry, with no time for thought, pushing forward and trying to outstrip their neighbours; but in the country it seems that things are different. Intellectual people live quiet, thoughtful, and even dreamy lives. They get through somehow without seeing the necessity for doing something—trying to be something that their neighbours cannot be—and no doubt they are happier for it. I am beginning to see how they are content to go on with their uneventful lives from year to year until the end even comes without a shock.'

'But you yourself would never reach that stage, Christian.'

'No, no, Hilda. I can understand it in others, but for me it is different. I have tasted too deeply of the other life. I should get restless——'

'You are getting restless already,' she interrupted gravely, 'and you have not been here two days!'

They were interrupted by Sidney's clear whistle, and a moment later Molly came tripping down the path.

'Come along in,' she said; 'the old gentleman is going. I was just stealing away to join you when Sidney whistled.'

When Signor Bruno reached his home that evening, he threw his hat upon the table with some considerable force. His aged landlady, having left the lamp burning, had retired to bed. He sank into an arm-chair, and contemplated the square toes of his own boots for some moments. Then he scratched his head thoughtfully.

'Sacré nom d'un chien!' he muttered; 'where have I seen that face before?'

Signor Bruno spoke French when soliloquising, which was perhaps somewhat peculiar for an Italian. However proficient a man may be in the mastery of foreign tongues, he usually dreams and talks to himself in the language he learnt at his mother's knee. He may count fluently in a strange tongue, but he invariably works out all mental arithmetic in his own. Likewise he prays—if he pray at all—in one tongue only. On the other hand, it appears very easy to swear in an acquired language. Probably our forefathers borrowed each other's expletives when things went so lamentably wrong over the Tower of Babel. Still muttering to himself, Signor Bruno presently retired to rest with the remembrance of a young face, peculiarly and unpleasantly strong, haunting his dreams.

Shortly after Signor Bruno's departure, Christian happened to be left alone in the drawing-room with Hilda. He promptly produced from his pocket the leaf he had cut from a book earlier in the evening. Unfolding the paper, he handed it to her, and said :—

'Do you recognise that?'

She looked at it, and answered without hesitation—

'Signor Bruno!'

The drawing was slight, but the likeness was perfect. The face was in profile, and the reproduction of the intelligent features could scarcely have been more lifelike in a careful portrait. Christian replaced the paper in his pocket.

'You remember Carl Trevetz, at Paris,' continued he; 'his father belonged to the Austrian Embassy!'

'Yes, I remember him!'

'To-morrow I will send this to him, simply asking who it is.'

'Yes,—and then?'

'When the answer comes, Hilda, I will write on the outside of the envelope the name that you will find inside—written by Trevetz?'

For a moment she looked across the table at him with a vague expression of wonder upon her face.

'Even if you are right,' she said, ' will it affect us? Will it make us cease to look upon him as a friend?'

'I think so.'

'Then,' she said slowly, 'it has come. You remember now?'

'Yes; I remember now—but it may be a mistake yet. I would rather have my memory confirmed by Trevetz before telling you what I know—or think I know—about Bruno!'

Hilda was about to question him further when Molly entered the room, and the subject was perforce dropped.

The next morning there came a letter for Christian from Mr. Bodery. It was short, and not very pleasant.

'Dear Vellacott,—Sorry to trouble you with business so early in your holiday, but there has been another great row in Paris, as you will see from the papers I send you. It is hinted that the mob are mere tools in the hands of influential wire-pullers, and the worst of it is that they were armed with English rifles and bayonets of a pattern just superseded by the War Office. How these got into their hands is not yet explained, but you will readily see the gravity of the circumstance in the present somewhat strained state of affairs. Several of the "dailies" refer to us, as you will see, and express a hope that our "exceptional knowledge of French affairs" will enable us to throw some light upon the subject. Trevetz is giving us all the information he can gather; but, of course, he is only able to devote a portion of his time to us. He hints that there is plenty of money in the background somewhere, and that a strong party has got up the whole affair— perhaps the Church. We must have something to say (something of importance) next week, and with this in view I must ask you to hold yourself in readiness to go to Paris on receipt of a telegram or letter from me.

'Yours,

'C. C. BODERY.'

Christian folded the letter, and replaced it in the envelope. Suddenly his attention was attracted to the latter. Upon the back there was a rim round the adhesive portion, and within this the glaze was gone from the paper. The envelope had been tampered with by a skilful manipulator. If Mr. Bodery had been in the habit of using inferior stationery, no trace would have been left upon the envelope.

Christian slipped the letter into his pocket, and, glancing round, saw that his movements had passed unobserved.

'Anything new?' asked Sidney, from the head of the table.

'Well, yes,' was the reply. 'There has been a disturbance in Paris. I may have to go over there on receipt of a telegram from the office;' he stopped, and looked slowly round the table. Hilda's attention was taken up by her plate, upon which, however, there was nothing. He leant forward, and handed her the toast-rack. She took a piece, but forgot to thank him. 'I am sorry,' he continued simply, 'very sorry that the disturbances should have taken place just at this time.'

His voice expressed natural and sincere regret, but no surprise. This seemed to arouse Molly's curiosity, for she looked up sharply.

'You do not seem to be at all surprised,' she said.

'No,' he replied; 'I am accustomed to this sort of thing, you see. I knew all along that there was the chance of being summoned at any time. This letter only adds to the chance—that is all!'

'It is a great shame,' said Molly, with a

pout. 'I am sure there are plenty of people who could do it instead of you.'

Christian laughed readily.

'I am sure there are,' he replied, 'and that is the very reason why I must take the opportunities that fortune offers.'

Hilda looked across the table at him, and noted the smile upon his lips, the light of energy in his eyes. The love of action had driven all other thoughts from his mind.

'I suppose,' she said, conversationally, 'that it will in reality be a good thing for you if the summons does come.'

'Yes,' he replied, without meeting her glance; 'it will be a good thing for me.'

'Is that consolatory view of the matter the outcome of philosophy, or of virtue?' inquired Molly, mischievously.

'Of virtue,' replied Christian gravely, and then he changed the subject.

After breakfast he devoted a short time to the study of some newspaper cuttings inclosed in Mr. Bodery's letter. Then he suddenly expressed his determination of walking down to the village post office.

'I wish,' he said, 'to send a telegram, and to get some newspapers, which have no doubt come by the second post. After that you will be troubled no more about my affairs.'

'Until a telegram comes,' said Hilda quietly, without looking up from a letter she held in her hand. She received one daily from Farrar.

Christian glanced at her with his quick smile.

'Oh,' he said, 'I do not expect a telegram. It is not so serious as all that. In fact, it is not worth thinking about.'

'You have a most enviable way of putting

aside disagreeable subjects,' persisted Hilda,
' for discussion at a vague future period.'

Christian was steadily cheerful that morn
ing, imperturbably practical.

' That,' he said, ' is the outcome—not of
virtue—but of philosophy.   Will you come to
the post office with Stanley and me?   I am
sure there is no possible household duty to
prevent you.'

Together they walked through the peaceful fields.   Stanley never lingered long beside
them ; something was for ever attracting him
aside or ahead, and he ran restlessly away.
Christian could not help noticing the difference in Hilda's manner when they were alone
together.   The semi-sarcastic *badinage* to
which he had been treated lately was completely dropped, and her earnest nature was
allowed to show itself undisguised.   Still she
was a mystery to him.   He was by habit a

close observer, but her changing moods and humours were to him unaccountable. At times she would make a remark the direct contradiction of which was shining in her eyes, and at other times she remained silent when mere politeness would seem to demand speech. Who knows? Perhaps at all times and in all things they understood each other. When their lips were exchanging mere nothings—the very lightest and emptiest of conversational chaff—despite averted eyes, despite indifferent manner, their souls may have been drawn together by that silent bond of sympathy which holds through fair and foul, through laughter and tears, through life, and beyond death.

Christian was not in the habit of allowing himself to become absorbed by any passing thoughts, however deep they might be. His mind had adapted itself to the work required of it, as the human mind is ever ready to do. No deep meditating was required of it, but a quick grasp and a somewhat superficial treatment. Journalism is superficial, it cannot be otherwise; it must be universal and immediate, and therefore its touch is necessarily light. There is nothing permanent about it except the ceaseless throb of the printing-machine and the warm smell of ink. That which a man writes one day may be rendered useless and worthless the next, through no carelessness of his, but by the simple course of events. He must perforce take up his pen again and write against himself. He may be inditing history, and his words may be forgotten in twelve hours. There is no time for deep thought, even if such were required. He who writes for cursory reading is wise if he writes cursorily.

Mr. Bodery's communication in no manner

disturbed Christian. He was ready enough to talk and laugh, or talk and be grave, as Hilda might dictate, while they walked side by side that morning, but she was strangely silent. It thus happened that little passed between them until they reached the post office. There, he was formally introduced to the spry little postmistress, who looked at him sharply over her spectacles.

'I wish, Mrs. Chalder,' he said cheerily, as he scribbled off his message to Mr. Bodery, while Hilda made friendly overtures to the official cat, 'I wish that you would forget to send me the disagreeable letters, and only forward the pleasant ones. There was one this morning, for instance, which you might very easily have mislaid. Instead of which you carefully sent it rather earlier than usual and spoilt my breakfast.'

His voice unconsciously followed the

swing of his pencil. It seemed certain that he was making conversation with the sole purpose of entertaining the old woman. With a pleased laugh and a shake of her grey curls she replied :

'Ah, I wish I could, sir. I wish I could burn the bad letters and send on only the good ones—but they're all alike on the outside. It's as hard to say what's inside a letter as it is to tell what's inside a man by lookin' on his face.'

'Yes,' replied Christian, reading over what he had just written. 'Yes, Mrs. Chalder, you are right.'

'But the reason of your letter gettin' earlier this morning was that Seen'yer Bruno said he was goin' past the Hall, sir, and would just leave the letters at the Lodge. It is a bit out of the carrier's way, and that man *do* have a long tramp every day, sir.'

'Ah, that accounts for it,' murmured the journalist, without looking up. He was occupied in crossing his t's and dotting his i's. He felt that Hilda was looking at him, and some instinct told him that she saw the motive of his conversation, but still he played his part and wore his mask of carelessness, as men have done before women, knowing the futility of it, since the world began. She never referred to the incident, and made no remark whatever with a view to his doing so, but he knew that it would be remembered, and in after days he learnt to build up a very castle of hope upon that frail foundation.

Hilda had not been paying much attention to what he was saying until Signor Bruno's name was mentioned. The old man had hitherto occupied a very secondary place in her thoughts. He was no one in her circle of possibly interesting people, beyond the fact of his having passed through a troubled political phase—a fighter on the losing side. Now he had, as it were, assumed a more important *rôle*. The mention of his name possessed a new suggestion; and all this, forsooth, because Christian Vellacott opined that the benevolent old face was known to him.

She began to entertain exaggerated ideas concerning the young journalist's thoughts and motives. Twice had she obtained a glimpse into the inner chamber of his mind, and on each occasion the result had been a vague suggestion of some mental conflict, some dark game of cross-purposes between him and Signor Bruno. Remembering this, she, in her intelligent simplicity, began to ascribe to Christian's every word and action an ulterior motive which in reality did not perhaps exist. She noted Christian's calm

and direct way of reaching the end he
desired, and unconsciously she yielded a little
to the influence of his strength—an influence
dangerously fascinating for a strong woman.
Her strength is so different from that of a
man that there is no real conflict—it seeks to
yield, and glories over its own downfall.

After paying for the telegram, Christian
took possession of the bulky packet of newspapers addressed to him, and they left the
post office.

CHAPTER X

ON THE SCENT

IT appeared to Stanley, on the way home that morning, that the conversation flagged somewhat. He therefore set to himself the task of reviving it.

'Christian,' he began conversationally. 'Is there any smuggling done now? Real smuggling, I mean.'

'No, I think not,' replied Christian. He evidently did not look upon smuggling as a fruitful topic at that moment.

'Why do you ask?' interposed Hilda good-naturedly.

'Well, I was just wondering,' replied the

boy. 'It struck me yesterday that our boat had been moved.'

'But,' suggested Christian, 'it should be very easy to see whether it has been dragged over the sand or not.'

'Three strong men could carry it bodily into the water and make no marks whatever on the sand,' argued little Stanley, determined not to be cheated out of his smugglers.

'Perhaps someone has been out for a row for his own pleasure and enjoyment,' suggested Christian, without thinking much of what he was saying.

'Then how did he get the padlock open?'

'Smugglers, I suppose,' said Hilda, smiling down at her small brother, 'would be provided with skeleton keys.'

'Of course,' replied Stanley in an awe-struck tone.

'I will tell you what we will do, Stanley,'

said Christian. 'To-morrow morning we will go and have a bathe; at the same time I will look at the boat and tell you whether it has been moved.'

'Unless,' added Hilda, 'a telegram comes to-day.'

Christian laughed.

'Unless,' he said gravely, 'the world comes to an end this evening.'

It happened during the precise moments occupied by this conversation, that Mr. Bodery, seated at his table in the little editor's room, opened the flimsy brown envelope of a telegram. He spread out the pink paper, and Mr. Morgan, seated opposite, raised his head from the closely-written sheets upon which his hand was resting.

'It is from Vellacott,' said the editor, and after a moment's thought he read aloud as follows :—

'Letter and papers received; believe I have dropped into the clue of the whole affair. Will write particulars.'

Mr. Morgan caressed his heavy moustache with the end of his penholder.

'That young man,' he said, 'goes about the world with his eyes remarkably wide open, ha-ha!'

Mr. Bodery rolled the telegram out flat with his pencil silently.

.   .   .   .   .

Stanley Carew was so anxious that the inspection of the boat should not be delayed, that an expedition to the Cove was arranged for the same afternoon. Accordingly the five young people walked across the bleak tableland together. Huge white clouds were rolling up from the south-west, obscuring every now and then the burning sun. A gentle breeze blew gaily across the bleak upland—a very different breath from that which twisted and gnarled the strong Scotch firs in winter-time.

'You would not care about climbing *down* there, I should think,' observed Sidney, when they had reached the Cove. 'It is a very different matter getting up.'

He was standing, gazing lazily up at the brown cliffs with his straw hat tilted backwards, his hands in his pockets, and his whole person presenting as fair a picture as one could desire of lazy quiescent strength— a striking contrast to the nervous, wiry townsman at his side.

'Hardly,' replied Christian, gazing upward at the dizzy height. 'It is rather nasty stuff—slippery in parts and soft.'

He turned and strolled off by Hilda's side. With a climber's love of a rocky height he looked upwards as they walked, and she noted the direction of his gaze.

Presently they sat on the edge of the boat over which Stanley's sense of proprietorship had been so grievously outraged.

'What do you know, Christian, or what do you suspect about Signor Bruno?' asked Hilda suddenly.

Stanley was running across the sands towards them, and Christian, seeing his approach, avoided the question by a generality.

'Wait a little longer,' he said. 'Let me have Trevetz's answer to confirm my suspicions, and then I will tell you. Suspicions are dangerous things to meddle with. In imparting them to other people it is so difficult to remember that they *are* suspicions and nothing more.'

At this moment Stanley arrived and threw himself down breathlessly on the warm sand.

'Chris!' he exclaimed, 'Come down

here and look at these seams in the boat—
the damp is there still.'

The boat was clinker-built, and where the
planks overlapped a slight appearance of
dampness was certainly discernible.   Christian lay lazily leaning upon his elbow, sometimes glancing at the boat in obedience to
Stanley's accusatory finger, sometimes looking
towards Hilda, whose eyes were turned sea-
wards.

Suddenly he caught sight of some words
pencilled on the stern-post of the boat, and
by the merest chance refrained from calling
Stanley's attention to them.   Drawing nearer,
he could read them easily enough.

Minuit vingt-six.

'It certainly looks,' he said rising, ' as if
the boat had been in the water, but it may be
that the dampness is merely owing to heavy
dew.   The boat wants painting, I think.'

He knew well enough that little Stanley's suspicions were correct. There was no doubt that the boat had been afloat quite recently ; but Christian knew his duty towards the ' Beacon ' and sacrificed his strict sense of truth to it.

On the way home he was somewhat pre-occupied—as much, that is to say, as he was in the habit of allowing. The pencil scrawl supplied food enough for conjectural thought. The writing was undoubtedly fresh, and this was the 26th of the month. Some appoint-ment was made for midnight by the words pencilled on the boat, and the journalist determined that he would be there to see. The question was, should he go alone? He watched Sidney Carew walking somewhat heavily along in front of him, and decided that he would not seek aid from that quarter. There was no time to communicate with Mr.

Bodery, so the only course open to him was to go by himself.

In a vague manner he had connected the Jesuit party with the disturbances in Paris and the importation of the English rifles wherewith the crowd had been armed. The gay capital was at that time in the hands of the most 'Provisional' and uncertain Government imaginable, and the home politics of France were completely disorganised. It was just the moment for the Church party to attempt a retrieval of their lost power. The firearms had been recognised by the English authorities as some of a pattern lately discarded. They had been stored at Plymouth, awaiting shipment to the colonies where they were to be served out to the auxiliary forces, when they had been cleverly removed. The robbery was not discovered until the rifles were found in the hands of a Paris mob, still fresh and brutal from the horrors of a long course of military law. Some of the more fiery of the French journals boldly hinted that the English Government had secretly sold the firearms with a view to their ultimate gain by the disorganisation of France.

Christian knew as much about affairs in Paris as most men. He was fully aware that in the politics of a disturbed country a deed is either a crime or a heroism according to circumstances, and he was wise enough to await the course of events before thrusting his opinion down the public throat. But now he felt that the crisis had supervened, and unwillingly he recognised that it was not for him to be idle amidst those rapid events.

These thoughts occupied his mind as he walked inland from the Cove, and rendered his answers to Stanley's ceaseless flow of questions upon all conceivable subjects somewhat vague and unreliable. Hilda was walking with them, and divided with Christian the task of supplying her small brother with varied information.

As they were approaching the Hall, Christian discerned two figures upon the smooth lawn, evidently coming towards them. At the same moment Stanley perceived them.

'I see Fred Farrar and Mr. Signor Bruno,' he exclaimed.

Christian could not resist glancing over the little fellow's head towards Hilda, though he knew that it was hardly a fair action. Hilda felt the glance but betrayed no sign. She was looking straight in front of her with no change of colour, no glad smile of welcome for her stalwart lover.

'I wonder why she never told me,' thought Christian.

Presently he said, in an airy, conversational way : 'I did not know Farrar was coming back so—so soon.'

He knew that by this early return Farrar was missing an important day of the race-meeting he had been attending, but did not think it necessary to remark upon the fact.

'Yes,' replied Hilda. 'He does not like to leave his mother for many days together.' The acutest ears could have detected no lowering of the voice, no tenderness of thought. She was simply stating a fact ; but she might have been speaking of Signor Bruno, so cool and unembarrassed was her tone.

'I am glad he is back,' said Christian thoughtlessly. It was a mere stop-gap. The silence was awkward, but he possessed tact enough to have broken it by some better means. Instantly he recognised his mistake, and for a moment he felt as if he were stumbling blindfold through an unknown country. He experienced a sudden sense of vacuity as if his mind were a blank and all words futile. It was now Stanley's turn to break the silence, and unconsciously he did it very well.

'I wonder,' he said speculatively, 'whether he has brought any chocolate creams?'

Hilda laughed, and the smile was still hovering in her eyes when she greeted the two men. Stanley ran on into the house to open a parcel which Farrar told him was awaiting inspection. It was only natural that Hilda should walk on with the young squire, leaving Bruno and Christian together. The old man lingered obviously, and his companion took the hint readily enough, anticipating some enjoyment.

'To you, Mr. Vellacott,' said the Italian, with senile geniality, 'to you whose life is spent in London this must be very charming, very peaceful and—very disorganising, I may perhaps add.'

Christian looked at his companion with grave attention.

'It is very enjoyable,' he replied simply.

Signor Bruno mentally trimmed his sails, and started off on another tack.

'Our young friends,' he said, indicating with a wave of his expressive hand Hilda and Farrar, 'are admirably suited to each other. Both young, both handsome, and both essentially English.'

'Yes,' answered Christian, with a polite display of interest; 'and, nevertheless, the Carews were all brought up and educated in France.'

'Ah!' observed the old man, stopping to raise the head of a 'Souvenir de Malmaison,' of which he inhaled the odour with evident pleasure. The little ejaculation, and its accompanying action, were admirably calculated to leave the hearer in doubt as to whether mere surprise was expressed or polite acquiescence in the statement of a known fact.

'Yes,' added Christian, deliberately. He also stooped and raised a white rose to his face, thus meeting Signor Bruno upon his own ground. The Italian looked up, and the two men smiled at each other across the rose bush; then they turned and walked on.

'You also know France,' hazarded Signor Bruno.

'Yes; if I were not an Englishman I should choose to be a Frenchman.'

'Ah!'

'Yes.'

'Now with me,' said Signor Bruno, frankly, ' it is different. If I were not an Italian (which God forbid!) I think—I think, yes, I am sure, I would by choice have been born an Englishman.'

'Ah!' observed Christian, gravely, and Signor Bruno turned sharply to glance at his face. The young Englishman was gazing straight in front of him, earnestly, with no suspicion upon his lips of the incredulous smile which seemed somehow to have lurked there when he last spoke. The Italian turned away dissatisfied, and they walked on a few paces in silence, until he spoke again, reflectively :—

'Yes,' he said, 'there is a quality in the English character which to me is very praiseworthy. It is a certain directness of purpose. You know what you wish to do, and you proceed calmly to do it without stopping to consider what your neighbours may think of it. Now with the Gallic races—for I take this virtue of straightforwardness as Teutonic—

and in my own country especially, men seek to gain their ends by less open means.'

They were now walking up a gentle incline to the house, which was built upon the buried ruins of its ancient predecessor, and Signor Bruno was compelled to pause in order to gain breath.

'But,' interposed Christian softly, 'you are now talking not so much of the people as of the Church.'

Again the Italian looked sharply up, and this time he met his companion's eyes fixed quietly on his face. He shrugged his shoulders deprecatingly and spread out his delicate hands.

'Perhaps you are right,' he said, with engaging frankness. 'I am afraid you are. But you must excuse a little ill-feeling in a man such as I, with a past such as mine has been, and loving his country as I do.'

'I am afraid,' continued Christian, 'that foreigners find our bluntness very disagreeable and difficult to meet; but I know that they frequently misjudge us on the same account. It is to our benefit, so we cannot complain.'

'In what way do we misjudge you?' asked Signor Bruno genially. They were almost on the threshold of the drawing-room window, which stood invitingly open, and from which came the sounds of cups and saucers being mated.

'You give us credit for less intelligence than we in reality possess,' said Christian with a smile, as he stood aside to let his companion pass in first.

Whatever influences may have been at work among those congregated at the Hall during the half-hour or so occupied by afternoon tea, no sign appeared upon the surface.

Molly as usual led the chorus of laughter. Hilda smiled her sweet 'kittenish' smile. Signor Bruno surpassed himself in the relation of innocent little tales, told with a true southern 'verve' and spirit, while Fred Farrar's genial laugh filled in the interstices reliably. Grave and unobtrusive, Christian moved about among them. He saw when Molly wanted the hot water, and was invariably the first to detect an empty cup. He laughed softly at Signor Bruno's stories, and occasionally capped them with a better, related in a conciser and equally humorous manner. It was to him that Farrar turned for an encouraging acquiescence when one of his latest Newmarket anecdotes threatened to fall flat, and with it all he found time for an occasional spar with Signor Bruno, just by way of keeping that inquiring gentleman upon his guard

CHAPTER XI

BURY BLUFF

As Christian walked rapidly across the uneven turf towards the sea at midnight, his thoughts were divided between a schoolboy delight in the adventurous nature of his expedition and an uncomfortable sensation of surreptitiousness. He was not accustomed to this sort of work, and felt remarkably like a thief. If by some mischance his absence was discovered at the Hall, it would be difficult to account for it unless he played the part of a temporary lunatic. Fortunately his window communicated easily enough with the garden by means of a few stone steps, but visitors are

not usually in the habit of leaving their bed-
rooms in order to take the air at midnight.
Thinking over these things in his rapid and
rather superficial way, he unconsciously
quickened his pace.

The night was clear and starlit; the air
soft and very pleasant, with a faint breath of
freshness from the south-west. The moon
being well upon the wane would not rise for
an hour or more, but the heavens were
glowing with the gentler light of stars, and on
earth the darkness was of that transparent
description which sailors prefer to the
brightest moonlight.

Christian Vellacott had worked out most
problems in life for himself. Taken as a
whole, his solutions had been fairly successful
—as successful as those of most men. If his
views upon things in general were rather
photographic—that is to say, hard, with

clearly defined shadows—it was owing to his father's somewhat cynical training and to the absence of a mother's influence. Elderly maiden ladies, with sufficient time upon their hands to manage other people's affairs in addition to their own, complained of his want of sympathy, which may be read in the sense of stating that he neither sought theirs nor asked advice upon questions connected with himself. This self-reliance was the inevitable outcome of his life at home and at the office of the 'Beacon.' Admirable as it may be, independence can undoubtedly be carried to an unpleasant excess—unpleasant, that is, for home life. Women love to see their men-folk a trifle dependent upon them.

Christian was in the midst of a problem as he walked across the tableland that stretched from St. Mary Western to the sea. That problem absorbed more of his attention

than the home politics of France; it required
a more careful study than any article he had
ever penned for the 'Beacon.' It gave him
greater anxiety than Aunt Judy and Aunt
Hester combined. Yet it was comprised in a
single word. A single arm could encompass
the whole of it. The single word—Hilda.

Leaving the narrow road, he presently
struck the little pathway leading to the Cove.
Suddenly he stopped, and stood motionless.
There—not twenty yards from him—was the
still figure of a man. Behind Christian the
land rose gradually to some considerable
height, so that he stood in darkness, while
against the glowing sky the figure of this
watcher was clearly defined in hard outline.
Instinctively crouching down and seeking
the covert of a few low bushes, Christian
decreased the intervening distance by a few
yards. The faint hope that it might prove to

be a coastguard was soon dispelled. The
heavy clothing and loose thigh-boots were
those of a fisherman. The huge 'cache-nez'
which lay in coils upon his shoulders and
completely protected the neck and throat,
was such as is worn by the natives of the
Côtes-du-Nord.

The sea boomed forth its melancholy
song, far down in the black depths beyond.
The tide was high, and the breeze freshening
every moment. Christian could have crept
up to the man's very feet without being
detected. Lying still upon the short dry
grass he watched for some moments.

From the man's clumsy attitude it was
almost possible to divine his slow mindless
nature—for there is expression in the very
turn of a man's leg as he stands—and it was
easy to see that he was guarding the little
path down the cliff to the Cove. He had

been posted there, and evidently meant to stay till called away.

There was only one way, now, to the Cove, and that was down the face of the cliff: the way that Christian had that very afternoon pronounced so hazardous. By day it was dangerous enough; by night it was almost an impossibility.

He crept noiselessly along to the eastward, so that the watcher stood upon the windward side of him, and reaching the brink he peered over into the darkness. Of course he could discern nothing. The sea rose and fell with a monotonous roar; overhead the stars twinkled as merrily as they have twinkled over the strifes of men from century to century.

Quietly he knelt upright and buttoned his coat with some care. Then without a moment's hesitation he crept to the edge and cautiously

disappeared into the grim abyss of darkness.
Slowly and laboriously he worked his way
down, feeling for each foothold in advance.
Occasionally he muttered impatiently to himself at the slowness of his progress. He knew
that the strata of soft sandstone trended downwards at an easy angle, and with consummate
skill took full advantage of his knowledge.
Occasionally he was forced to progress sideways with his face to the rock and hands out-
stretched till his fingers were cramped, and
the feeling known as 'pins and needles' as-
sailed his arms. Then he would rest for some
moments, peering into the darkness below
him all the while. Once or twice he dropped
a small stone cautiously, holding it at arm's
length. When the tiny messenger touched
earth soon after leaving his hand, he continued
his downward progress. Once, no sound
followed for some seconds, and then it was

only a distant concussion far down beside the sea. With an involuntary shudder, the climber turned and made his way upwards and sideways again, before venturing to descend once more.

For half an hour he continued his perilous struggle, till his strong arms were stiff and his fingers almost powerless. With marvellous tenacity he held to his purpose. Never since leaving the summit had he been able to rest both hands at once. With a dogged mechanical endurance which is essential y characteristic of climbers and mountaineers, he lowered himself, inch by inch, foot by foot. Louder and louder sang the sea, as if in derision at his petty efforts, but through his head there rushed another sound infinitely more terrible: a painful continuous buzz, which seemed to press upon his temples. A dull pain was slowly creeping up the muscles of his neck towards his head. All these symptoms the climber knew. The buzzing in his ears would never cease until he could lie down and breathe freely with every muscle relaxed, every sinew slack. The dull ache would creep up until it reached his brain, and then nothing could save him—no strength of will could prevent his fingers from relaxing their hold.

'Sish—sish, sish—sish!' laughed the waves below. Placidly the stars held on their stately course—each perhaps peopled by millions of its own—young and old, tame and fiery—all pursuing shadows as we do here.

'This is getting serious,' muttered Christian with a pitiful laugh. The perspiration was running down his face, burning his eyes, and dripping from his chin. With straining eyes he peered into the night. Close beneath him there was a ledge of some breadth. It was not flat, but inclined upwards from the face of the cliff, thus forming a shelf of solid stone. For some seconds he stared continuously at this, so as to reduce to a minimum the chance of being mistaken. Then with great caution he slid down the steep incline of smooth stone and landed safely. The glissade lasted but a moment, nevertheless it recalled to his mind a picture which was indelibly stamped in his memory. Years before he had seen a man slide like this, unintentionally, after a false step. Again that picture came to him—unimpressionable as his life had rendered him. Again he saw the glittering expanse of snow, and on it the broad strong figure of the Vaudois guide sliding down and down, with madly increasing speed—feet foremost, skilful to the last. Again he felt the thrill which men cannot but experience at the sight of a man, or even of a dumb beast, fighting

bravely for life.   Again he saw the dull gleam
of the uplifted ice-axe as the man dealt
scientific blow after blow on the frozen snow,
attempting to arrest his terrible career.   And
again in his mind's eye the pure expanse of
spotless white lay before him, scarred by one
straight streak, marking where the taciturn
mountaineer had vanished over the edge of
the precipice to his certain doom.

Christian lay like a half-drowned man upon
the shelving ledge, slowly realising his position.
He calculated that he could not yet be half-way
down, and his strength was almost exhausted.
Yet, as he lay there, no thought of waiting
for daylight, no question of retreat entered
his stubborn West-country brain.   The ex-
ploit still possessed for him the elements of a
good joke, to be related thereafter in such a
manner as would enforce laughter.

Suddenly—within the softer sound of the

sea below—a harsh grating noise struck his
ears.   It was to him like the sound made by
a nailed boot upon rock.   It was as if another
were following him down the face of the cliff.
In a second he was upon his feet, his weariness a thing forgotten.   Overhead, against the
starlit sky, he could define the line of rock
with its sharp, broken angles and uncouth
turns.   Not thirty feet above him something
was moving   His first feeling was one of
intense fear.   Every climber knows that it is
easier to pass a difficult corner than to stand
idle, watching another do it.   Slowly the dark
form came downwards, and suddenly, with a
quick sense of unutterable relief, Christian
saw the black line of a tightened rope.   When
it was barely ten feet above him he saw that
the object was no man, but a square case.   In
a flash of thought he divined what the box
contained, and unhesitatingly ran along the

ledge towards it. As it descended he seized it with both hands and swung it in towards himself. With pendulum-like motion it descended, and at last touched the rock at his feet. As this took place he grasped the rope with both hands and threw his entire weight upon it, hauling slowly in, hand over hand. So quickly and deftly was this carried out that those lowering overhead were deceived, and continued to pay out the rope slowly. Steadily Christian hauled in, the slack falling in snake-like coils at his feet. Only being able to guess at his position on the cliff, it was no easy matter to calculate how much rope it was necessary to take in in order to carry out the deception.

At length he ceased abruptly, and proceeded to untie the knots round the bale. Then, after the manner of a sailor who is working out of sight with a life-line, he jerked the rope, which immediately began to ascend

rapidly and with irregularity. Coil after coil
ran easily away, and at last the frayed end
passed into the darkness above Christian's
head. He stood there watching it, and when
it had disappeared he burst into a low hoarse
laugh which suddenly broke off into a sicken-
ing gurgle, and he fell sideways and backwards on to the box, clutching at it with
his nerveless fingers.

When he recovered his faculties his first
sensation was one of great cold. The breeze
had freshened with the approach of dawn,
and blowing full upon him as he lay bathed in
perspiration, the effect was like that of a
refrigerator. He moved uneasily, and found
that he was lying on the stone ledge *outside*
the box from which he had fallen. After a
moment, he rose rapidly to his feet as if
desirous of dismissing the memory of his
own collapse, and turned his attention to the

bundle. Beneath the rough covering of canvas, which was not sewn but merely lashed round, it was easy enough to detect the shape of the case.

'What luck—what wonderful luck,' he muttered, as he groped round the surface of the bundle.

Indeed it seemed as if everything had arranged itself for his special benefit and advantage.

The three men whose duty it had been to lower the case coiled up their rope and started off on foot inland, after telling the sentinel stationed at the head of the little path to rejoin his boat. This the man was only too willing to do at once. He was a semi-superstitious Breton of no great intelligence, who vastly preferred being afloat in his unsavoury yawl to climbing about unknown rocks in the dark. On the beach, he found

his two comrades, to whom he gruffly imparted the information that they were to go
on board.

'Had the "monsieur" said nothing else?'

'No, the "monsieur" said nothing else.'

The Breton intellect is not, as a rule,
acute. Like sheep the three men proceeded
to carry up from the water's edge Stanley's
boat, which was required to carry the heavy
case, their own dinghy being too small.
This done, they rowed off silently to the
yawl, which was rolling lazily in the trough
of the sea, a quarter of a mile from the
shore. Once on board they were regaled
with some choice French profanity from the
lips of a large man in a sealskin cap and a
dirty woollen muffler. This gentleman they
addressed as the 'patron,' and, with clumsy
awe, informed him that they had waited at the
same spot as before, but nothing had come,

until at length Hoel Grall arrived with instructions from the 'monsieur' to go on board. Whereupon further French profanity, followed by unintelligible orders, freely interlarded with embellishments of a forcible tenor.

As the yawl swung slowly round and stood out to sea, Christian turned to climb up Bury Bluff. He found that he had in reality made very little progress in descending. Before leaving the case, he edged it by degrees nearer to the base of the ledge, which would render it invisible from the beach. The ascent was soon accomplished, and after a cautious search he concluded that no one was about, so set off home at a rapid pace.

Before he reached the Hall the light of coming day was already creeping up into the eastern sky. All Nature was stirring refreshed with the balmy dew and coolness of the night. Far up in the higher branches of the Weymouth pines the wrens were awake, calling to each other with tentative twitter, and pluming themselves the while for another day of sunshine and song.

Like a thief Christian hurried on, and creeping into his bedroom window, was soon sleeping the dreamless forgetful sleep of youth.

By seven o'clock he was awake with all the quick realisation of a Londoner. In the country men wake up slowly, and slowly gather together their senses after an all-sufficing sleep of ten hours. In cities, five, four, or even three are sufficient for the unfatigued body and the restless mind. Men wake up quickly, and are at once in full possession of their faculties. It is, after all, a mere matter of habit.

Christian had slept sufficiently. He rose

quite fresh and strong, and presently sat down, coatless, to write.

Page after page he wrote, turning each leaf over upon its face as it was completed— never referring back, never hesitating, and only occasionally raising his pen from the paper. Line after line of neat small writing, quite different from what his friends knew in letters or on envelopes, flowed from his pen. It was his 'press' handwriting, plain, rapid, and as legible as print. The punctuation was attended to with singular care: the commas broad and heavy, the colons like the kisses in a child's letter, round and black. Once or twice he smiled as he wrote, and occasionally jerked his head to one side critically as he re-read a sentence.

In less than two hours it was finished. He rose from his seat, and walked slowly to the window. Standing there he gazed

thoughtfully across the bare unlovely tableland towards the sea. He had written many
hundreds of pages, all more or less masterly;
he had read criticisms upon his own work
saying that it was good; and yet he knew
that the best—the best he had ever written—
lay upon the table behind him. Then he
turned and shook the loose leaves together
symmetrically. Pensively he counted them.
He was young and strong; the world and
life lay before him, with their infinite possibilities—their countless opportunities to be
seized or left. He looked curiously at the
written pages. The writing was his own;
the form of every letter was familiar; the
heavy punctuation and clean, closely-written
lines such as the compositor loved to deal
with; and while he turned the leaves over he
wondered if ever he would do better, for he
knew that it was good.

CHAPTER XII

A WARNING WORD

As the breakfast-bell echoed through the house, Christian ran downstairs. He met Hilda entering the open door with the letters in her hand.

'Down already?' he exclaimed.

'Yes,' she replied incautiously, 'I wished to get the letters early.'

'And after all, there is nothing for you?'

'No,' she replied. 'No, but ——'

She stopped suddenly and handed him two letters, which he took slowly, and apparently forgot to thank her, saying nothing at all. There was a peculiar expression of dawning surprise upon his face, and he studied the envelopes in his hand without reading a word of the address. Presently he raised his eyes and glanced at Hilda. She was holding a letter daintily between her two forefingers, cornerwise, and with little puffs of her pouted lips was spinning it round, evidently enjoying the infantile amusement immensely.

He dropped his letters into the pocket of his jacket, and stood aside for her to pass into the house ; but she, abruptly ceasing her windmill operations, looked at him with raised eyebrows and stood still.

'Well ?' she said interrogatively.

'What ?'

'And Mr. Trevetz's answer—I suppose it is one of those letters ?'

'Oh yes !' he replied.   'I had forgotten my promise.'

He took the letters from his pocket, and looked at the addresses again.

'One is from Trevetz,' he said slowly, ' and the other from Mrs. Strawd.'

' Nothing from Mr. Bodery?' asked she indifferently.

He had taken a pencil from his pocket, and, turning, he held Trevetz's letter against the wall while he wrote across it. Without ceasing his occupation, and in a casual way, he replied :—

' No, nothing from Mr. Bodery ; so I am free as yet.'

'I am very glad,' she murmured conventionally.

'And I,' he said, turning with a polite smile to hand her the letter.

She took the envelope, and holding it up in both hands examined it critically.

'M a-x,' she read; 'how badly it is written! Max—Max Talma—is that it?'

'Yes,' he answered gravely, 'that is it.'

With a little laugh and a shrug of her shoulders she proceeded to open the envelope. It contained nothing but the sketch made upon the fly-leaf of a novel. Christian was watching her face. She continued to smile as she unfolded the paper. Then she suddenly became grave, and handed the open sketch to him. At the foot was written :—

'Max Talma—look out! Avoid him as you would the devil!
'In haste, C. T.'

Christian read it, laughed carelessly, and thrust the paper into his pocket. 'Trevetz writes in a good forcible style,' he said, turning to greet Molly, who came, singing, downstairs at this moment. For an instant her merry eyes assumed a scrutinising, almost anxious look as she caught sight of her sister and Christian standing together.

' Are you just down ?' she asked carelessly.

' Yes,' answered Christian, still holding her hand. 'I have just come down.'

As usual the day's pleasure was all pre-arranged. A groom rode to the station at Christian's request with a large envelope upon which was printed Mr. Bodery's name and address. This was to be given to the guard, who would in his turn hand it to a special messenger at Paddington, and the editor of the 'Beacon' would receive it by four o'clock in the afternoon.

The day was fine with a fresh breeze, and the programme of pleasure was satisfactorily carried out. But with sunset the wind freshened into a brisk gale, and heavy clouds rolled upwards from the western horizon. This was the first suggestion of autumn, the first sigh of dying summer. The lamps were lighted a few minutes earlier that night, and the family assembled in the drawing-room soon after dark, although the windows were left open for those who wished to pass in and out.

Mrs. Carew's grey head was, as usual, bent over some simple needlework, while Molly sat near at hand. According to her wont she also was busy, while around her the work lay strewed in picturesque disorder. Sidney was reading in his own room—reading for a vague law examination which always appeared to have been lately postponed till next October.

Christian was seated at the piano, playing by snatches and turning over the brown leaves of some very old music, unearthed from a lumber-room by Mrs. Carew for his benefit. He waited for no thanks or comment; some-

times he read a few bars only, sometimes a
page. He appeared to have forgotten that he
had an audience. Presently he rose, leaving
the music in disorder. Hilda had been called
away some time before by an old village
woman requiring medicaments for unheard-of
symptoms. Christian looked slowly round
the room, then raising his hand he dexterously
caught a huge moth which had flown past his
face.

As he crossed the room towards the open
window, with a view of liberating the moth,
a low whistle reached his ear. The refrain
was that of the familiar 'retraite.' Hilda had
evidently gone out to the moat by another
door. Bowing his head, he passed between
the muslin curtains and disappeared in the
darkness. The sound of his footsteps died
away almost immediately amidst the rustle of

branch and leaf already crisp with approaching change.

It was Stanley's bed-time. Mechanically, Molly kissed her brother, continuing to work thoughtfully.

In a few minutes the door opened and Hilda entered the room. She came up to the table, and standing there with her hands resting upon some pieces of Molly's work, she gave a graphic description of the old woman's complaints and maladies. She stood quite close to Molly, and told her story to Mrs. Carew merrily, failing to notice that her sister had ceased sewing, and was listening with a surprised look in her eyes. When the symptoms had been detailed and laughed over, Hilda turned quietly and passed out into the garden. With fearless familiarity she ran lightly down the narrow pathway towards the moat, but no signal-whistle greeted her. The leaves rustled

and whispered overhead; the water lapped
and gurgled at her feet, but there was no sign
or sound of life.

Silent and motionless she stood, a tall fair
form clad in white, amidst the universal darkness. So silent and so still that it might have
been the shade of some fair maid of bygone
years mourning the loss of her true knight,
who in all the circumstances of war had
crossed that same moat never to return.

Presently a sudden feeling of loneliness, a
new sense of fear, came over Hilda. All
around was so forbidding. The water at her
feet was so black and mysterious. She gave
a soft low whistle identical with that which had
called Christian out twenty minutes before,
but it remained unanswered, and through the
rustling leaves she sped towards the house.
From the open window a glow of rosy light
shone forth upon the flowers, imparting to all

alike a pallid pink, and dimly defining the grey tree-trunks across the lawn. As Hilda stepped between the curtains, the servants entered the drawing-room in solemn Indian file for evening prayers.

Mrs. Carew looked up from the Bible which lay open before her, and said to Hilda :—

'Where is Christian?'

'I don't know, mother; he is not in the garden,' answered the girl, crossing the room to her own particular chair.

Sidney rose from his seat, and going to the window, sent his loud clear whistle away into the night. His broad figure remained motionless for some minutes, almost filling up the window; then he silently resumed his seat.

Mrs. Carew smoothed down the silken book-marker, and began reading in a low voice. It is to be feared that the Psalmist's words of joy were not heard with understanding ears that night. A short prayer followed; softly and melodiously Mrs. Carew asked for blessings upon the bowed heads around her, and the servants left the room.

'Have you not seen Christian since you went to see Mrs. Sender, Hilda?' asked Molly, at once.

'No,' replied Hilda, arranging the music into something like order upon the piano.

'He went out about half an hour ago, in answer to your whistle.'

Hilda turned her head as if about to reply hastily, but checked herself, and resumed her task of setting the music in order.

'How could I whistle,' she asked gently, 'when I was in the kitchen doling out medicated cotton-wool to Mrs. Sender?'

Molly looked puzzled.

'Did *you* whistle, Sidney?' she asked.

'I—no; I was half-asleep over a law-book in my own room.'

'I expect he has gone for a stroll, and forgotten the time,' suggested Mrs. Carew reassuringly, as she sat down to work again.

'But what about the whistle; are you sure you heard it, Molly?' asked Hilda, speaking rather more quickly than was habitual with her. She walked towards the window and drew aside the curtain, keeping her back turned towards the room.

'Yes,' answered Molly uneasily. 'Yes—I heard it, and so did he, for he went out at once.'

Sidney stood awkwardly with his shoulder against the mantelpiece, listening in a half-hearted way to his sisters' conversation. With a heavy jerk he threw himself upright and slowly crossed the room. He stood for some moments immediately behind Hilda without touching her. Then he raised his hand and with gentle, almost caressing pressure round her waist, he made her step aside so that he could pass out. He was a singularly undemonstrative man, rarely giving way to what he considered the weakness of a caress. Fortunately, however, for their own happiness, his womenfolk understood him, and especially between himself and Hilda there existed a peculiar unspoken sympathy.

In the ordinary way, he would have mumbled—

' Le'mme out ! '

On this occasion he touched her waist gently, and the caress almost startled her. It seemed like a confession that he shared the vague anxiety which she concealed so well.

With the charity of maternal love, which

is by no means so blind as is generally supposed, Mrs. Carew often said of Sidney that he invariably rose to the occasion; and Mrs. Carew's statements were as a rule correct. His slowness was partly assumed; his indifference was a mere habit. The assumption of the former saved him infinite worry and responsibility; the habit of indifference did away with the necessity of coming to a decision upon general questions. This state of mind may, to townsmen, be incomprehensible. Certain it is that such as are in that condition are not found among the foremost dwellers in cities. But in the country it is a different matter. Such cases are only too common, and (without breath of disparagement) they are usually to be found in households where one man finds himself among several women —be the latter mother and sisters, or wife and sisters-in-law.

The man may be a thorough sportsman, he may be an excellent landlord and a popular squire, but within his own doors he is overwhelmed. Chivalry bids him give way to the wishes and desires of some woman or other, and if he be a sportsman he is necessarily chivalrous. When one is tired after a long day in the saddle or with a gun, it is so much easier to acquiesce and philosophically persuade oneself that the matter is not worth airing an adverse opinion over. This is the beginning, and if any beginning can look forward to great endings it is that of a habit.

It would appear that Sidney Carew's occasion had come at last, for once outside the window he changed to a different being. The lazy slouch vanished from his movements, his eyes lost their droop, and he held his head erect.

He made his way rapidly to the stable,

and there, without the knowledge of the grooms, he obtained a large hurricane-lamp, lighted it, and returned towards the house. From the window Hilda saw him pass down a little path towards the moat, with the lamp swinging at his side, while the shadows waved backwards and forwards across the lawn.

The mind is a strange storehouse. However long a memory may have been warehoused there, deep down beneath piles of other remembrances and conceits, it is generally to be found at the top when the demand comes, ready for use—for good or evil. A dim recollection was resuscitated in Sidney's mind. An unauthenticated nursery tale of a departing guest leaving with a word of joy upon his lips and warm comfort in his heart, turning from the glowing doorway and walking down the little pathway straight into the moat.

Christian, however, was an excellent swimmer; he knew every inch of the pathway, every stone round the moat. That he should have been drowned in ten feet of clear water, with an easy landing within ten yards, seemed the wildest impossibility. Of course such things have happened, but Christian Vellacott was essentially wide awake, and unlikely to come to mishap through his own carelessness.

Of all these things Sidney thought as he walked rapidly towards the moat, and in particular he pondered over Molly's statement that she had heard Hilda whistle. This had met with flat denial from Hilda, and Sidney with brotherly candour could only arrive at the conclusion that Molly had been mistaken. He would not give way to the least suggestion of anxiety even in his own mind. After all Christian would probably come in with some simple explanation and a laugh for their fears. It often happens thus, as we must all know. The moments so long and dreary for the watcher, whose imagination gains more and more power as the time passes, slip away unheeded by the awaited, who treats the matter with a laugh or, at the most, a few conventional words of sympathy.

Sidney stood at the edge of the water and threw the beams of light across the rippling surface. Mechanically he followed the ray as it swept from end to end of the moat, and presently, without heeding, he turned his attention to the stones at his feet. A gleam of reflected light caught his passing gaze, and he stooped to examine the cause more closely.

The smooth stonework was wet; in fact the water was standing in little pools upon it. Round these there were circles of dampness, showing that evaporation was taking place. The water had not lain there long. A man falling into the moat would have thrown up splashes such as these; in no other way could they be plausibly accounted for.

Sidney stood erect. Again he held the lamp over the gleaming water, half fearing to see something. His lips had quite suddenly become dry and parched, and there was an uncomfortable throb in his throat. Suddenly he heard a rustle behind him, and before he could draw back Hilda was at his side. She slipped her hand through his arm, and by the slightest pressure drew him away from the moat.

'You know—Sid—he could swim perfectly,' she said persuasively.

He made no answer, but walked slowly by her side, swinging the lamp backwards and forwards as a schoolboy swings his satchel.

Thus he gained time to moisten his lips and render speech possible.

Together they went round the grounds, but no sign or vestige of Christian did they discover. A pang of remorse came to Hilda as she touched her brother's strong arm. Ever since Christian's arrival she remembered that Sidney had been somewhat neglected, or only remembered when his services were required. Christian had indeed been attentive to him, but Hilda felt that their friendship was not what it used to be. The young journalist in his upward progress had left the slow-thinking country squire behind him. All they had in common belonged to the past ; and, for Christian, the past was of small importance compared to the present. She recollected that during the last fortnight everything had been arranged with a view to giving pleasure to herself, Molly, and Christian, without heed to Sidney's inclinations. By word or sign he had never shown his knowledge of this; he had never implied that his existence or opinion was of any great consequence. She remembered even that such pleasures as Christian had shared with Sidney—pleasures after his own heart, sailing, shooting, and fishing—had been undertaken at Christian's instigation or suggestion, and eagerly welcomed by Sidney.

And now, at the first suspicion of trouble, she turned instinctively to her brother for the help and counsel which were so willingly and modestly accorded.

'Sidney,' she said, 'did he ever speak to you of his work?'

'No,' he replied slowly; 'No, I think not.'

'He has been rather worried over these disturbances in Paris, I think, and—and—I suppose he has never said anything to you about Signor Bruno?'

'Signor Bruno!' said Sidney, repeating the name in some surprise. 'No, he has never mentioned his name to me.'

'He does not like him——'

'Neither do I.'

'But you never told me—Sid!'

'No,' he replied, simply; 'there was nothing to be gained by it!'

This was lamentably true, and Hilda felt that it was so, although her brother had no thought of posing as a martyr.

'Christian,' she continued softly, 'distrusted him for some reason. He knows something of his former life, and told me a short time ago that Bruno was not his name at all. This morning Christian received a letter from Carl Trevetz, whom we knew in Paris, you will remember, saying that Signor

Bruno's real name was Max Talma, also warning Christian to avoid him.'

'Is this all you know?' asked Sidney, in a peculiarly quiet tone.

'That is all I know,' she replied. 'But it has struck me that—that *this* may have something to do with Signor Bruno. I mean —is it not probable that Christian may have discovered something which caused him to go away suddenly without letting Bruno know of his departure?'

Sidney thought of the water at the edge of the moat. The incident might prove easy enough of explanation, but at the moment it was singularly unreconcilable with Hilda's comforting explanation. And again, the recollection of the signal whistle heard by Molly was unwelcome.

'Yes,' he replied, vaguely. 'Yes, it may.'

He was, by nature and habit, a slow

thinker, and Hilda was running away from him a little; but he was, perhaps, surer than she.

'I am convinced, Sidney,' she continued, 'that Christian connects Signor Bruno in some manner with the disturbances in France. It seems very strange that an old man buried alive in a small village should have it in his power to do so much harm.'

'A man's power of doing harm is practically unlimited,' he said slowly, still wishing to gain time.

'Yes, but he has always appeared so child-like and innocent.'

'That is exactly what I disliked about him,' said Sidney.

'Then do you think he has been deliberately deceiving us all along?' she asked.

'Not necessarily,' was the tolerant reply. 'You must remember that Christian is essentially a politician. He does not suspect Bruno of anything criminal; his suspicions are merely political; and it may be that Bruno's doings, whatever they appear to be now, may in the future be looked upon as the actions of a hero. Politics are impersonal, and Signor Bruno is only known to us socially.'

Hilda could not see the matter in this light. No woman could have been expected to do so.

'I suppose,' she said, presently, 'that Signor Bruno is a political intriguer.'

'I expect so,' replied her brother.

They were walking slowly up the broad path towards the house, having given up the idea of searching for Christian or calling him.

'Then,' continued Sidney, 'you think it is likely that he has gone off to see Bruno, or to watch him?'

'I think so.'

'That is the only reasonable explanation I can think of,' he said, gravely and doubtfully, for he was still thinking of the moat.

They entered the house, and to Mrs. Carew and Molly their explanation was imparted. It was received somewhat doubtfully, especially by Molly. However, the farce had to be kept up—and do we not act in similar comedies every day?

CHAPTER XIII

A NIGHT WATCH

CHEERFULNESS is, thank goodness, infectious. The watchers at the Hall that night made a great show of light-heartedness. Sidney had risen to the occasion. He laughed at the idea of anything serious having happened to Christian, and his confidence gradually spread and gained new strength. Molly, however, was apparently beyond its influence. With her perpetual needle-work in her hands she sat beneath the lamp and worked rapidly. Occasionally she glanced towards Hilda, but contributed nothing to the explanations forth-coming from all quarters.

Hilda was also working; slowly, however, and with marvellous care. She was engaged upon a more artistic production than ever came from Molly's work-basket. Once she consulted Mrs. Carew about the colour of a skein of wool, but otherwise showed no inclination to avoid topics in any manner connected with Christian, despite the fact that these were obviously distasteful to her family. In all that she said, indifference was blended in a singular way with imperturbable cheerfulness.

Thus they waited until after midnight, pretending bravely to work and read as if there were no such feeling as suspense in the human heart. Then Mrs. Carew persuaded the young people to go to bed. She had letters to write, and would not be ready for hours. If Christian did not appear by the time that she was sleepy, she would wake

Sidney. After all, she acted her part better than they. She was old at it—they were new. She was experienced in stage-craft and made her points skilfully; above all, she did not over-act.

The three young people kissed their mother and left the room, assuring each other of their conviction that they would find Christian at the breakfast table next morning. Molly's room was at the head of the stairs. With a smile and a nod she closed her door while Hilda and Sidney walked slowly down the long passage together. Arrived at the end, Sidney kissed his sister. She turned the handle of her door and stood with her back to him for a few moments without entering the room, as if to give him an opportunity of speaking if he had aught to say. He stood awkwardly behind her, gazing mechanically at her hair, which reflected the light from the candle that he was holding all awry, while the wax dripped upon the carpet.

'It will be all right, Hilda,' he said unevenly, 'never fear!'

'Yes, dear, I know it will,' she replied.

And then she passed into the room without closing the door, and he walked on with loudly-creaking shoes.

Hilda crossed her room and set the candle upon the dressing-table. She waited there till Sidney's footsteps had ceased, and then she turned and walked uprightly to the door, which she closed. She looked round the room with a strange vacant look in her eyes, and then she made her way unsteadily towards the bed, where she lay staring at the wavering candle and its reflection in the mirror behind until daylight came to make its flame grow pale and yellow.

There were four watchers in the house

that night. Downstairs, Mrs. Carew sat by the shaded lamp in her upright armchair. She was not writing, but had re-opened the large black Bible. Molly was courting sleep in vain, having resolutely blown out her candle. Sidney made no pretence. He was fully dressed, and seated at his rarely-used writing-table. Before him lay a telegraph-form bearing nothing but the address—

C. C. Bodery, 'Beacon' Office, Fleet St., London.

He was gazing mechanically at the blank spaces waiting to be filled in, and through his mind was passing and repassing the same question that occupied the thoughts of his mother and sisters. What could be the explanation of the whistle heard by Molly? The want of this alone sufficed to overthrow the most ingenious of consolatory explanations. All four looked at it from different points of

view, and to each the signal-whistle calling
Christian into the garden was an insurmount-
able barrier to every explanation.

Before it was wholly light Hilda moved
wearily to the window. She threw it open,
and sat with arms resting on the sill and her
chin upon her hands, mechanically noting the
wonders of the sunrise. A soft white mist
was rising from the thick pasture, wholly
obscuring the sea and filling the atmosphere
with a damp chill. Seated there in her thin
evening dress, she showed no sign of feeling
the cold. At times physical pain is almost a
pleasure. The glistening damp rested on
every blade of grass, on every leaf and twig,
while the many webs stood whitely against the
shadows, some hanging like festoons from tree
to tree, others floating out in mid-air without
apparent reason or support. In and among
the branches lingered little secret deposits

of mist waiting the sun's warmth to melt them all away.

The suppressed creak of Sidney's door attracted Hilda's attention, but she did not move, merely turning to look at her own door as her brother passed it with awkward caution. A dull instinct told her that he was going to the moat again. Presently he passed beneath her window and across the dewy lawn, leaving a trailing mark upon the grass. The whole picture seemed suddenly to be familiar to her. She had lived through it all before—not in another life, not in years gone by, not in a dream, but during the last few hours.

The air was very still, and she could hear the clank of the chain as Sidney unmoored the old punt, rarely used except by the gardener to clean the moat when the weeds died down in autumn. The quiet was rendered more remarkable by the suddenness of its advent. All night it had been blowing a wild gale, which dropped at dawn, and from the soft land the mist rose instantly.

Prompted by a vague desire to be doing something, Hilda presently turned from the window, and, after a moment's indecision, chose from the shelf a novel fresh from the brain of the king of writers. With it she returned to her low chair and listlessly turned over the leaves for some moments. She raised her head and sought in vain the tiny form of a lark trilling out his morning hymn far up in the blue sky. Then she resolutely commenced to read uninterruptedly.

She read on until Sidney's firm step upon the gravel beneath the window roused her. A minute later he knocked softly at her door. The water was glistening on his rough shooting-boots as he entered the room, and upon the brown leather gaiters there was a deeper shade showing where the wet grass had brushed against his legs. His honest immobile face showed but little surprise at the sight of Hilda still in evening dress, but she saw that he noticed it.

She rose from her low chair and laid aside the book, but no sort of greeting passed between them.

'I have been all round again,' he said quietly, 'by daylight, and—and of course there is no sign.'

She nodded her head, but did not speak.

'I have been thinking,' he continued, somewhat shyly, 'as to what is to be done. First of all, no one must be told. Mother, Molly, you, and I know it, and we must keep it to ourselves. We will tell Stanley that Christian has gone off suddenly in connection with his work, and the same excuse will do for the neighbours and servants. I will telegraph this morning to Mr. Bodery, the editor of the "Beacon," and await his instructions.   I think that is all that we can do in the meantime.'

She was standing close to him, with one hand on the table, resting upon the closed volume of 'Vanity Fair,' but instead of looking at her brother she was gazing calmly out of the window.

'Yes,' she murmured, 'I think that is all that we can do in the meantime.'

Sidney moved awkwardly as if about to leave the room, but hesitated still.

'Have you nothing to suggest?' he asked. 'Do you think I am acting rightly?'

She was still looking out of the window— still standing motionless near the table with her hand upon Thackeray's 'Vanity Fair.'

'Yes,' she replied; 'everything you suggest seems wise and prudent.'

'Then will you see mother and Molly in

their rooms and forewarn them to say nothing—nothing that may betray our anxiety ? '

' Yes, I will see them.'

Sidney walked heavily to the door. Grasping the handle, he turned round once more.

' It is nearly half-past seven,' he said with more confidence in his tone, ' and Mary will soon be coming to awake you. It would not do for her to see you in that dress.'

Hilda turned and raised her eyes to his face.

' No,' she said with a sudden smile ; ' I will change it at once.'

CHAPTER XIV

FOILED

WHEN Mr. Bodery opened the door of the room upon the second floor of the tall house in the Strand that morning, he found Mr. Morgan seated at the table surrounded by proof-sheets, with his coat off and shirt-sleeves tucked up. The sub-editor of the 'Beacon' was in reality a good hard worker in his comfortable way, and there was little harm in his desire that the world should be aware of his industry.

'Good morning, Morgan,' said the editor, hanging up his hat.

'Morning,' replied the other, genially, but

without looking up. Before Mr. Bodery had seated himself, however, the sub-editor laid his hand with heavy approval upon the odoriferous proof-sheet before him, and looked up.

'This article of Vellacott's is first-rate,' he said. 'By Jove! sir, he drops on these holy fathers—lets them have it right and left. The way he has worked out the thing is wonderful, and that method of putting everything upon supposition is a grand idea. It suggests how the thing *could* be done upon the face of it, while the initiated will see quickly enough that it means to show how the trick was in reality performed—ha, ha!'

'Yes,' replied Mr. Bodery absently. He was glancing at the pile of letters that lay upon his desk. There were among them one or two telegrams, and these he put to one side while he took up each envelope in succession to examine the address, throwing it down again unopened. At length he turned again to the telegrams, and picked up the top one. He was about to tear open the envelope when there was a sharp knock at the door.

' 'M'in ! ' said Mr. Morgan sharply, and at the same moment the silent door was thrown open. The diminutive form of the boy stood in the aperture.

' Gentleman to see you, sir,' he said with great solemnity.

' What name ? ' asked Mr. Bodery.

' Wouldn't give his name, sir—said you didn't know it, sir.'

Even this small office-boy was allowed his quantum of discretionary power. It rested with him whether an unknown visitor was admitted or politely dismissed to a much greater extent than anyone suspected. Into

his manner of announcing a person he somehow managed to convey his opinion as to
whether it was worth the editor's time to
admit him or not, and he invariably received
Mr. Bodery's 'Tell him I am engaged' with a
little nod of mutual understanding which was
intensely comprehensive.

On this occasion his manner said, 'Have
him in—have him in, my boy, and you will
find it worth your while!'

'Show him in,' said Mr. Bodery.

The nameless gentleman must have been
at the door upon the boy's heels, for no
sooner had the words left Mr. Bodery's lips
than a tall dark form slid into the room. So
noiseless and rapid were this gentleman's
movements that there is no other word with
which to express his mode of progression.

He made a low bow, and shot up erect
again with startling rapidity. He then stood

quietly waiting until the door had closed behind the small boy, who, after having punctiliously expectorated upon a silver coin which had found its way into the palm of his hand, proceeded to slide down the balustrade upon his waistcoat.

It often occurred that strangers addressed themselves to Mr. Morgan when ushered into the little back room, under the impression that he was the editor of the 'Beacon.' Not so, however, this tall, clean-shaven person. He fixed his peculiar light-blue eyes upon Mr. Bodery, and, with a slight inclination, said suavely,—

'This, sir, is, I believe, your printing day?'

'It is, sir, and a busy day with us,' replied the editor, with no great warmth of manner.

'Would it be possible now,' inquired the

stranger conversationally, 'at this late hour, to remove a printed article and substitute another?'

At these words Mr. Morgan ceased making some pencil notes with which he was occupied, and looked up. He met the stranger's benign glance and, while still looking at him, deliberately turned over all the proof-sheets before him, leaving no printed matter exposed to the gaze of the curious.

Mr. Bodery had in the meantime consulted his watch.

'Yes,' he replied, with dangerous politeness. 'There would still be time to do so if necessary—at the sacrifice of some hundred-weight of paper.'

'How marvellously organised your interesting paper must be!'

Dead silence. Most men would have felt embarrassed, but no sign of such feeling was forthcoming from any of the three. It is possible that the dark gentleman with the sky-blue eyes wished to establish a sense of embarrassment with a view to the furtherance of his own ends. If so, his attempt proved lamentably abortive. Mr. Bodery sat with his plump hands resting on the table, and looked contemplatively up into the stranger's face. Mr. Morgan was scribbling pencil notes on a tablet.

' The truth is,' explained the stranger at length, ' that a friend of mine, who is unfortunately ill in bed this morning——'

(Mr Bodery did not look in the least sympathetic, though he listened attentively.)

'. . . . has received a telegram from a gentleman who I am told is on the staff of your journal—Mr. Vellacott. This gentleman wishes to withdraw, for correction, an article he has sent to you. He states that he will re-write the article, with certain alterations, in time for next week's issue.'

Mr. Bodery's face was pleasantly illegible.

' May I see the telegram?' he asked politely.

' Certainly !'

The stranger produced and handed to the editor a pink paper covered with faint black writing.

' You will see at the foot this—Mr. Vellacott's reason for not wiring to you direct. He wished my friend to be here before the printers got to work this morning ; but owing to this unfortunate illness——'

' I am afraid you are too late, sir,' interrupted Mr. Bodery briskly. ' The press is at work——'

' My friend instructed me,' interposed the stranger in his turn, ' to make you rather a difficult proposition. If a thousand pounds will compensate for the loss incurred by the delay of issue, and defray the expense of paper spoilt—I—I have that amount with me.'

Mr. Bodery did not display the least sign of surprise, merely shaking his head with a quiet smile. Mr. Morgan however laid aside his pencil, and placed his elbow upon the proof-sheets before him.

The stranger then stepped forward with a sudden change of manner.

'Mr. Bodery,' he said in a low concentrated voice, 'I will give you five hundred pounds for a proof copy of Mr. Vellacott's article.'

A dead silence of some moments' duration followed this remark. Mr. Morgan raised his head and looked across the table at his chief. The editor made an almost imperceptible motion with his eyebrows in the direction of the door.

Then Mr. Morgan rose somewhat heavily from his chair, with a hand upon either arm, after the manner of a man who is beginning to put on weight rapidly. He went to the door, opened it, and, turning towards the stranger, said urbanely—

'Sir—the door!'

This kind invitation was not, at once, accepted.

'You refuse my offers,' said the stranger curtly, without deigning to notice the sub-editor.

Mr. Bodery had turned his attention to his letters, of which he was cutting open the envelopes, one by one, with a paper-knife, without however removing the contents. He looked up.

'To-morrow morning,' he said, 'you will be able to procure a copy from any stationer for the trifling sum of sixpence.'

Then the stranger walked slowly past Mr. Morgan out of the room.

'A curse on these Englishmen!' he muttered as he passed down the narrow staircase. 'If I could only see the article I could tell whether it is worth resorting to stronger measures or not. However, that is Talma's business to decide, not mine.'

Mr. Morgan closed the door of the small room and resumed his seat. He then laughed aloud, but Mr. Bodery did not respond.

'That's one of them,' observed Mr. Morgan comprehensively.

'Yes,' replied the editor, 'a dangerous customer. I do not like a blue-chinned man.'

'I was not much impressed with his diplomatic skill.'

'No; but you must remember that he had difficult cards to play. No doubt his information was of the scantiest, and—we are not chickens, Morgan.'

'No,' said Mr. Morgan, with a little sigh. He turned to the revision of the proof-sheets again, while the editor began opening and reading his telegrams.

'This is a little strong,' exclaimed Mr. Morgan, after a few moments of silence, broken only by the crackle of paper. 'Just listen here' :—

'It simply comes to this—the General of the Society of Jesus is an autocrat in the worst sense of the word. He holds within his fingers the wires of a vast machine moving with little friction and no noise. No farthest corner of the world is entirely beyond its influence; no political crisis passes that is not hurried on or restrained by its power. Unrecognised, unseen even, and often undreamt of, the vast Society does its work. It is not for us who live in a broad-minded, tolerant age to judge too harshly. It is not for us to say that the Jesuits are unscrupulous and treacherous. Let us be just and give them their due. They are undoubtedly earnest in their work, sincere in their belief, true to their faith. But it is for us to uphold our own integrity. We are accused—as a nation—of stirring up the seeds of rebellion, of crime and bloodshed in the heart of another country. Our denial is considered insufficient; our evidence is ignored. There remains yet to us one mode of self-defence. After denying the crime (for crime it is in humane and political sense) we can turn and boldly lay it upon those whom its results would chiefly benefit: the Roman Catholic Church in general—the Society of Jesus in particular. We have endeavoured to show how the followers of Ignatius Loyola could have brought about the present crisis in France; the extent to which they would benefit by a religious re-action is patent to the most casual observer; let the Government of England do the rest.'

Mr. Bodery was, however, not listening. He was staring vacantly at a telegram which lay spread out upon the table.

'What is the meaning of this?' he exclaimed huskily.

The sub-editor looked up sharply, with his pen poised in the air. Then Mr Bodery read:

'Is Vellacott with you? Fear something wrong. Disappeared from here last night.'

Mr. Morgan moved in his seat, stretching one arm out, while he pensively rubbed his clean-shaven chin and looked critically across the table.

'Who is it from?' he asked.

'Sidney Carew, the man he is staying with.'

They remained thus for some moments: the editor looking at the telegram with a peculiar blank expression in his eyes; Mr. Morgan staring at him while he rubbed his chin thoughtfully with outspread finger and thumb. In the lane beneath the window some industrious housekeeper was sweeping her doorstep with aggravating monotony; otherwise there was no sound.

At length Mr. Morgan rose from his seat and walked slowly to the window. He stood gazing out upon the smoke-begrimed roofs and crooked chimneys. Between his lips he held his pen, and his hands were thrust deeply into his trouser pockets. It was on that spot and in that attitude that he usually thought out his carefully written weekly article upon 'Home Affairs.' He was still there when the editor touched a small gong which stood on the table at his side. The silent door instantly opened, and the supernaturally sharp boy stood on the threshold grimly awaiting his orders.

'Bradshaw.'

'Yess'r,' replied the boy, closing the door. His inventive mind had conceived a new and improved method of going downstairs. This was to lie flat on his back upon the balustrade with a leg dangling on either side. If the balance was correct, he slid down rapidly and shot out some feet from the bottom, as he had, from an advantageous point of view on Blackfriars Bridge, seen sacks of meal shoot from a Thames warehouse into the barge beneath. If, however, he made a miscalculation, he inevitably rolled off sideways and landed in a heap on the floor. Either result appeared to afford him infinite enjoyment and exhilaration. On this occasion he performed the feat with marked success.

'Guv'nor's goin' on the loose—wants the
railway guide,' he confided to a small friend
in the printing interest whom he met as he
was returning with the required volume.

'Suppose you'll be sitten' upstairs now,
then,' remarked the black-fingered one with
fine sarcasm. Whereupon there followed a
feint—a desperate lunge to one side, a
vigorous bob of the head, and a resounding
bang with the railway guide in the centre of
the sarcastic youth's waistcoat.

Having executed a strategic movement,
and a masterly retreat up the stairs, the small
boy leant over the banisters and delivered
himself of the following explanation—

'I 'it yer one that time.   Don't do it agin!
Good morning, Sir.'

Mr. Bodery turned the flimsy leaves impatiently, stopped, looked rapidly down a
column, and, without raising his eyes from

the railway guide, tore a telegraph form from the handle of a drawer at his side. Then he wrote in a large clear style :—

'Will be with you at five o'clock. Invent some excuse for V's absence. On no account give alarm to authorities.'

The sharp boy took the telegram from the editor's hand with an expression of profound respect upon his wicked features.

'Go down to Banks,' said Mr. Bodery, 'ask him to let me have two copies of the foreign policy article in ten minutes.'

When the silent door was closed, Mr. Morgan wheeled round upon his heels and gazed meditatively at his superior.

'Going down to see these people?' he asked, with a jerk of his head towards the West.

'Yes, I am going by the eleven fifteen.'

'I have been thinking,' continued the sub-editor, 'we may as well keep the printing-office door locked to-day. That slippery gentleman with the watery eyes meant business, or I am very much mistaken. I'll just send upstairs for Bander to go on duty at the shop door to-day as well as to-morrow; I think we shall have a big sale this week.'

Mr. Bodery rose from his seat and began brushing his faultless hat.

'Yes,' he replied; 'do that. It would be very easy to get at the machinery. Printers are only human!'

'Machinery is ready enough to go wrong when nobody wishes it,' murmured Mr. Morgan vaguely, as he sat down at the table and began setting the scattered papers in order.

Mr. Bodery and his colleagues were in the habit of keeping at the office a small bag, containing the luggage necessary for a few nights in case of their being suddenly called

away. This expedient was due to Christian
Vellacott's forethought.

The editor now proceeded to stuff into his
bag sundry morning newspapers and a large
cigar case. Telegraph forms, pen, ink, and
foolscap paper were already there.

'I say, Bodery,' said the sub-editor with
grave familiarity. 'It seems to me that you
are taking much too serious a view of this
matter. Vellacott is as wide-awake as any
man, and it always struck me that he was
very well able to take care of himself.'

'I have a wholesome dread of men who
use religion as a means of justification. A
fanatic is always dangerous.'

'A sincere fanatic,' suggested the sub-
editor.

'Exactly so; and a sincere fanatic in the
hands of an agitator is the very devil. That
is whence these fellows get their power.

Half of them are fanatics and the other half hypocrites.'

Mr. Bodery had now completed his preparations, and he held out his plump hand, which the sub-editor grasped.

'I hope,' said the latter, 'that you will find Vellacott at the station to meet you, ha, ha!'

'I hope so.'

'If,' said Mr. Morgan, following the editor to the door, 'If he turns up here, I will wire to Carew and to you, care of the station-master.'

END OF THE FIRST VOLUME

PRINTED BY
SPOTTISWOODE AND CO., NEW-STREET SQUARE
LONDON

www.ingramcontent.com/pod-product-compliance
Lightning Source LLC
Chambersburg PA
CBHW031347070726
47496CB00017B/1815